Donald MacKenzie and The Murder Room

〉〉〉 This title is part of The Murder Room, our series dedicated to making available out-of-print or hard-to-find titles by classic crime writers.

Crime fiction has always held up a mirror to society. The Victorians were fascinated by sensational murder and the emerging science of detection; now we are obsessed with the forensic detail of violent death. And no other genre has so captivated and enthralled readers.

Vast troves of classic crime writing have for a long time been unavailable to all but the most dedicated frequenters of second-hand bookshops. The advent of digital publishing means that we are now able to bring you the backlists of a huge range of titles by classic and contemporary crime writers, some of which have been out of print for decades.

From the genteel amateur private eyes of the Golden Age and the femmes fatales of pulp fiction, to the morally ambiguous hard-boiled detectives of mid twentieth-century America and their descendants who walk our twenty-first century streets, The Murder Room has it all. **〉〉〉**

The Murder Room
Where Criminal Minds Meet

themurderroom.com

Donald MacKenzie 1908–1994

Donald MacKenzie was born in Ontario, Canada, and educated in England, Canada and Switzerland. For twenty-five years MacKenzie lived by crime in many countries. 'I went to jail,' he wrote, 'if not with depressing regularity, too often for my liking.' His last sentences were five years in the United States and three years in England, running consecutively. He began writing and selling stories when in American jail. 'I try to do exactly as I like as often as possible and I don't think I'm either psychopathic, a wayward boy, a problem of our time, a charming rogue. Or ever was.'

He had a wife, Estrela, and a daughter, and they divided their time between England, Portugal, Spain and Austria.

Henry Chalice

Salute from a Dead Man
Death Is a Friend
Sleep Is for the Rich

John Raven

Zalenski's Percentage
Raven in Flight
Raven and the Kamikaze
Raven and the Ratcatcher
Raven After Dark
Raven Settles a Score
Raven and the Paperhangers

Raven's Revenge
Raven's Longest Night
Raven's Shadow
Nobody Here By That Name
A Savage State of Grace
By Any Illegal Means
The Eyes of the Goat
The Sixth Deadly Sin
Loose Cannon

Standalone novels

Nowhere to Go
The Juryman
The Scent of Danger
Dangerous Silence
Knife Edge
The Genial Stranger
Double Exposure
The Lonely Side of the River
Cool Sleeps Balaban
Dead Straight
Three Minus Two
Night Boat from Puerto Vedra
The Kyle Contract
Postscript to a Dead Letter
The Spreewald Collection
Deep, Dark and Dead
Last of the Boatriders

Dead Straight

Donald MacKenzie

An Orion book

Copyright © The Estate of Donald MacKenzie 1968

The right of Donald MacKenzie to be identified as the author of this
work has been asserted in accordance with the Copyright, Designs and
Patents Act 1988.

This edition published by
The Orion Publishing Group Ltd
Orion House
5 Upper St Martin's Lane
London WC2H 9EA

An Hachette UK company
A CIP catalogue record for this book is available from the British Library

ISBN 978 1 4719 0577 3

www.orionbooks.co.uk

For my daughter Kirstie whose unexpected arrival would suggest she will have a nice sense of humour and timing

Monday

A GROUP OF Flower People had invaded the corner of King's Road. They stood in the drizzle, jangling their bells, handing out wilted daisies to the passers-by. A man with a ginger beard and a dirty caftan snuffled a message as I pushed by.

"Open the body to ecstasy, friend. Communicate."

I walked north of Manresa Road. It was only early afternoon but the Polytechnic classrooms were ablaze with light. The new steel-and-concrete towers nipped the dome of Chelsea Public Library like a nut ready for cracking.

Bicycles were chained to the railings outside the dreary building. I went up the steps, avoiding the prams, the stiff-legged airedale in the lobby. I could have gone through the entire building with my eyes closed. Over the last week, I'd spent as much time in it as out.

The Reference Room was left and up the stairs, past the mimeographing machine, the posters advertising night classes. Immediately in front was the Lending Library. Spectacled girls sat behind the counter, checking books in and out. Women in wet macs browsed through the shelves in an atmosphere reminiscent of a Methodist chapel. There was the same reverent hush, the cautious coughs and squeaks of rub-

1

ber soles on linoleum. The same smell of oil fumes and floor polish.

The Reading Room was empty, the day's batch of newspapers spread on the stands. The building was warm and I knew where the staff defied the NO SMOKING signs. I draped my trench coat over a radiator to dry and opened the *Daily Telegraph*. I've never been able to work out who pays for the printed texts that always head the Personal Column. The day's offering was ambiguous: *AND his mercy is on them that fear him from generation to generation.* St. Luke 1:50.

I might as well explain what I was doing in the library. To me it seemed simple. I was looking for a job. Newspapers advertise jobs. The library bought the newspapers. Not that I qualified as the guy most likely to succeed. There was a small matter of a police record. I'd served time for jewel theft in Canada, France, and England. In fact it was eleven months to the day since my release. My last sentence had been three years. The judge at the Central Criminal Court accompanied it with a warning — the next sentence would be considerably longer. As far as I was concerned, the advice was superfluous. I'm not suggesting that I'd left the dock trying on a halo for size. All that happened was that I'd been shaken into thinking of the future.

I'd always believed that the dividing line between rogue and successful businessman was an arbitrary one. I still believed it. I just didn't relish rotting in jail for the next ten years, trying to prove the premise. The other reason was Kirstie Kirkpatrick.

More about Kirstie. She'd stood my bail, dealt with unpaid bills and reporters, stored my clothes for me. Even more

2

importantly she'd sat in court, close to the dock where I could see her. They'd given us five minutes alone together, afterwards — in a room underneath the court. She did the talking, pulling no punches. She left nothing to doubt. What she'd done for me, she said, had been done for love. The rest was up to me. I gave her the answer she wanted. Neither of us ever referred to it again directly.

All through the two years of waiting, she visited me faithfully. She was my only correspondent. She was outside the gates the morning of my release, a job already lined up for me. Clerk in a Kensington travel bureau. I started the following morning. The owner was an old friend of Kirstie's, Bill Gaynor. She'd told him about my past — she was that sort of girl. Gaynor leaned over backwards to show his broadmindedness — he was that sort of guy. So I sold tickets all through the long dreary winter. Tickets for Caribbean cruises, holidays on safari, East African sunshine. I booked diamond-studded matrons into hotels that I remembered with nostalgic envy.

I walked off the job one Monday morning, leaving Gaynor owing me two weeks' money. I thought it evened things out. Not Kirstie. She harangued me for the best part of an hour, about ingratitude — a lack of responsibility. The implication was that I'd failed her. I hadn't realized you put on gratitude, like a clean shirt, shining and fresh every day. She let it be known that from then on I could find my own jobs. So I did. I hawked fire-fighting appliances door-to-door. This lasted three weeks. I learned more about the failings of men over forty than the Gallup Poll has. But I only made two sales. One didn't really count. It turned out that the woman

3

was deaf and greeted the follow-up from the head office with a threat to go to the police. I handed in my satchel and collected my insurance cards.

A stint on a construction gang followed, with me competing with bucks from the Irish bogs. That didn't work out either. I still saw Kirstie, eating at her flat most evenings. The job syndrome had developed into a sort of running battle between us — obstinacy on her part, exasperation on mine. I guess I must have turned up for fifty interviews, April through July. Each time a prospective employer asked for a work history, I gave him the truth. The record included six months picking apples. Springfield Prison Farm, Ontario. Nine months as button-maker, Fresnes Prison, France. Two years in Winchester Prison, floor-washer and librarian.

The reactions varied from the get-out-of-here-you-bum to reluctant amusement. The final decision was the same in every case. I was virtually unemployable. Kirstie's accusations were furious. I was cynical and aggressive; how could I expect people to respond? Just the way they had, I answered. She couldn't have it both ways. For the next six weeks I ran a power shovel in a sandpit outside Slough. The only people who worried about my record were the local police. There was gelignite stored at the pit. Someone had a word with the management. I was fired the next day. Since then I'd been drawing a weekly handout from the National Assistance Board. The mechanics of the procedure are not calculated to heighten the applicant's self-respect. I'd thought of the alternative frequently. But the reasons against that were still valid.

I thumbed down the list of boxed advertisements. Titled

ladies offered their flats while they wintered abroad. Public school boys undertook to do anything legal. People made assignations. Suddenly I saw it.

WANTED *Man of resource and courage to act as companion. Excellent salary. Telephone Central 0049.*

I tore the page out and folded it carefully. I grabbed my coat and hurried out to the nearest pay booth. I dialed the number given. A girl gave me directions in a ho-hum voice that suggested she'd done the same thing, already too often. Mr. Pardoe would see me at four-thirty. She wasted no more time on me. The address was of a firm of solicitors.

I looked at my watch. It was almost three. My first impulse was to call Kirstie and tell her. Her office was only minutes away from where I was going. She worked as a copywriter in an advertising agency. But I'd sounded too many false alarms already.

I made it back home through the drizzle. Gainsborough Studios was housed in a terra-cotta-fronted building on the corner of Fulham Road. A spade-bearded painter with a Hungarian accent lived in the top apartment. The next down was someone called Harvey Gribble, a buyer in the rag-trade. Below him was his girlfriend, a harpy built on the order of a gunboat. The bottom flat was mine. I opened the door and shut it behind me.

The house agent had described the place as a "compact studio apartment suitable for a single girl or bachelor, comfortably furnished and with access to a charming garden." There was one large room with an erection of bamboo poles from floor to ceiling screening off the kitchen unit. Plastic greenery dotted with large wax camelias wound round the poles. The bed was up a couple of steps on a platform. A nylon drape hid it during the day. There was a fair-sized clothes closet, four chairs and a table. That was it. The only decoration on the wall was a blown-up picture of Kirstie. The television set belonged to her. A door behind the refrigerator opened into the yard. To reach it you stood sideways, moving like a crab. A complicated maneuver that got you nowhere. All that was outside were four garbage cans.

The rent was thirty-two pounds a month, lighting and heating inclusive, telephone extra. I'd hit lucky back in July with a long shot at the races. The bookmaker's check insured that at least I had a roof until the end of the year. The furnace room was directly underneath my apartment, the oil-fired heating system operated by a time-switch. The owner's agent visited the building every Saturday, setting the time-switch and temperature to his liking. I'd made a key to fit the door below. As soon as the agent left, I turned the heating on full blast, resetting it early on the morning before his visit. If the exercise was illegal, it didn't bother me.

I opened a window and went into the bathroom. I stripped, dumping shirt, socks and shorts in the tub to soak. A man living alone evolves time-saving routines without even thinking about it. I could take care of the household chores while the coffee was brewing. First I made the bed, then jockeyed the Hoover round the carpet. Next came garbage disposal, yesterday's refuse wrapped in yesterday's newspaper and dumped in the yard. By this time the coffee had perked. I'd reached the stage where I could wash a shirt, half-dry it on the radiator and iron it in thirty-five minutes flat. This satisfied me and irritated Kirstie. It was an area in which she preferred to think of me as being helpless.

The living room windows overlooked Fulham Road. Plastic-wrapped pedestrians tangled umbrellas in shop doorways. Buses sailed down the street, spraying slush over the sidewalks. For no reason at all, I remembered a half-hoop of beach, the rhythmic movement of a horse galloping under me, the sweet smell of orange blossoms in the early Moroccan sunshine.

I read the piece of newsprint again, imagination soaring with lunatic optimism. *Resource and courage.* For five seconds, the scene was lifted out of a Hitchcock movie — the door opening at the end of a mirrored corridor, the shadowed room where a man behind a desk waited for me. If I'd had any sense at all I'd have taken six ounces of scotch and gone straight to bed.

Instead, I readied myself for the interview. There were half a dozen suits hanging in the closet. A couple of drawers full of shirts and ties, five pairs of shoes with trees. Everything I owned would have fitted into two good-sized bags. The thought knocked some of the bounce out of me. I chose a gray flannel suit, black shoes, and knitted silk tie. I shut the window and turned off the lights. The afternoon mail lay on the hall mat. The one postcard from Majorca was for Gribble. I left it where it was. He wasn't my favorite person. I didn't have to calculate how much cash I had in my pocket. It was Monday. I took a bus to South Kensington subway station, surfacing at the Temple. It was twenty past four. I knew the neighborhood well — the narrow streets of gloomy houses where lawyers lurked in Dickensian rooms. The address I wanted was at the end of King's Bench Walk. The front door was opposite a railed-off stretch of soaked grass. Beyond that was the river.

Wet footmarks tracked the uncarpeted floor. I read the name on the brass plate:

Edward Pardoe & Co.
Solicitors
Privy Council Agents
Commissioners for Oaths
Edward Pardoe, D.D.L.

I pushed the door, taking off my trench coat. A girl looked up from a desk. I gave her my name. She blocked a yawn, checking a list in front of her. Her nod indicated a door on my right. The room had one large window, horsehair chairs round a solid black table. Four men were there ahead of me. I carried a copy of the *Law Review* to a chair by the window. My name had been last on the list. I took a good look at the opposition. The two men sitting at the table had regimental haircuts, blazers with army badges, trousers with deep cuffs. Each had the gimlet-eyed stare of a drill sergeant. The man standing in front of the fireplace was a superior version of the same breed. A major's mustache bristled under a fleshy nose. He wore a small blue flower in the lapel of his checked jacket. He rocked on well-shod heels, his attitude making it plain that the rest of us were wasting our time. He exuded a strong smell of gin and looked slightly drunk. The last competitor was either Maltese or Cypriot. He'd brought his own reading material. He concentrated on it, breathing heavily through a flattened nose. Hair like black wire sprouted from his ears. I could only suppose that he thought he was in a gymnasium.

We sat in the prickly threat of silence, staring at one another furtively, rain dripping outside the window. I was on the point of leaving when a couple came in from the street. The man was the Identikit lawyer, in his early sixties. White-haired and tweeded, still handsome in the Barrymore tradition. The woman was dressed in a simple black suit. She could have been any age between thirty and forty. Medium height, blond, with good bones and the fine skin that went with her coloring. The man with her pulled a door. I heard her voice as she went through to an inner office — well-bred with an undertone of nervousness. She looked at none of us.

A secretary poked her head round the door of the reception office.

"Mr. Purser, please. Will you go through?"

The major thumbed up his mustache, settled his jacket, and vanished. He was out in a few minutes. He swayed slightly, pausing to address us.

"Doomed, the lot of you," he said distinctly, belched, and slammed the door behind him.

The others were in and out almost as rapidly. Any or none of them might have been hired. It was impossible to tell from their expressions. I sat there alone till the girl gave the signal. I left my trench coat on the chair and followed her into the warm room. The man at the desk was leaning on his elbows, a pair of heavy-framed spectacles dangling between his fingers. He indicated the chair in front of him.

"This is Mrs. Straight, Mr. Bain. My name is Pardoe."

I sat down. Leatherbound lawbooks were ranged against the paneled walls. There was a safe on a pedestal in the corner, an atmosphere of secrets expensively guarded. I glanced across at the woman sitting in the window. Her back was to the street. She was watching me through a wreath of cigarette smoke, her legs crossed at the knees. One heel was free of its patent leather pump. She wore a plain gold band on the third finger of her left hand, a sapphire-and-diamond clip on her tailored jacket. Ash-blond hair reached to her shoulders. It was the last year she'd be able to wear it that long.

Pardoe tapped the tape recorder in front of him. "I hope you don't mind," he said casually. "It's just that it saves time."

I shook my head. He touched a switch. The tapes started to revolve.

"Let me tell you why you're here," Pardoe explained. "Mrs. Straight's looking for someone who will live in the house with her. A sort of companion. The pay is forty pounds a week with a guarantee of three months."

I waited for the rest but Pardoe leaned back, masking his chin in his hand.

"A sort of companion?" I repeated. "Can't you be a little more explicit than that?"

Pardoe stared at the ceiling. My first thought was: an attractive woman, wealthy — hired help required to deal with an unwanted lover. I looked at Mrs. Straight, and decided I was wrong.

"Why *did* you answer the advertisement, Mr. Bain?" she asked courteously. No finesse. Just a straight hard ball over the middle of the plate.

"Does there have to *be* a special reason?" I asked. "I needed a job."

She considered my answer and appeared to give me benefit of the doubt.

"Then what work *do* you do?" she persisted.

"You name it and I've done it," I smiled. "But right now I'm unemployed."

Pardoe swung round in his chair. She flicked the ash from her holder nervously. There was dead silence. I felt the tension between them. Pardoe cleared his throat.

"You're an American, I take it, Mr. Bain?"

I shook my head. "If you mean a citizen of the United States, no. I'm Canadian."

He leaned back, tapping the edge of the desk with a gold pencil. Mrs. Straight put the next question hesitantly. But her eyes didn't leave my face.

"Why does a man like you have to look for a job in a newspaper?"

I shrugged. "What did the others say — or didn't you ask them?"

Her cheeks colored slightly, teeth catching her lower lip. "I don't mean to be rude, Mr. Bain. I'm in a difficult position. Please try to understand."

Pardoe's wave rescued her from further embarrassment. "Why don't we find out whether his talents are what you're looking for, Jessica? What do you specialize in, Mr. Bain?"

I fished a package of butts from my pocket. I wondered what they'd say if I answered burglary. Candor seemed to work like a breeze with anyone but a prospective employer. Socially it could sink any attempt at pretension. *Last summer, Mrs. Burpington-Upwater? I wouldn't really know — I was in jail.* Someone would laugh, breaking the sudden hush and say how *amusing* it was. This seemed one of the

11

times when the truth ought to be sweetened with a little harmless lying.

I lined up the points of my shoes, looking down at them modestly.

"I've been a trainee in a racehorse stable. Deckhand on a Great Lakes tanker. I was in the export-import business in Tangier and I've been a sort of soldier."

Pardoe's remark was curious rather than unfriendly. "That's an odd thing, Jessica. Five applicants and four of them ex-servicemen."

"I wouldn't call myself an ex-serviceman," I said easily. "This was in the Congo. I was a mercenary for eighteen months, the last six without pay. I came here in April. The demand's light for my kind of soldiering." I'd no idea why I said it, beyond the fact that I thought it would discourage further inquiries.

Pardoe looked as if he thought otherwise. Mrs. Straight's gesture silenced him.

"For God's sake let someone else talk, Edward." She turned to me confidently. "Do you call yourself a judge of character, Mr. Bain?"

It was a loaded question and I hedged. "I guess that would depend on the subject. I've been known to be wrong."

She got up slowly, looking for an ashtray. "What about me?" she smiled. "Do I strike you as a neurotic woman?"

I looked at her twice before making up my mind that she was serious. She bent over, stubbing out her cigarette. The movement showed the cleft of her breasts, youthful and oddly touching.

"Neurotic, no. But I've got a hunch that you're scared."

She glanced sharply at Pardoe. "Then you've realized more than most people do, Mr. Bain."

Pardoe was watching me from behind the desk. He glanced away as I caught him.

"It's getting late," I reminded them. "I'd like to be back before the rush hour."

She was staring out at the rain-soaked street. She turned and picked up her gloves and handbag.

"I have the feeling you can help me, Mr. Bain. The point is, *will* you?"

Part of my brain said get up and go. But the money had hooked me. I spread my hands. "I came for a job."

She spoke to Pardoe. "I've made my mind up. You can take care of the rest. I'll call you in the morning."

She offered me her hand, smiling mechanically. "Mr. Pardoe will let you know whatever is necessary. I'll expect you tomorrow."

Pardoe showed her to the street. He came back, shutting the door carefully. He sat down behind the desk, still tapping with his gold pencil.

"I suppose you can supply references?" he asked suddenly.

There was an odd inflection in his voice. Almost as if he hoped I'd say no.

"The sort of life I've been leading," I replied. "You don't ask for references and you don't give them."

He scribbled my name on the pad. "A bank," he suggested. "A doctor or solicitor. Anyone who'll vouch for you. It's purely a formality, I can assure you. I know by now when Mrs. Straight has made up her mind."

I gave him two names. The first was Gerry Singleton at the

13

Ottawa office of the Canada Council. I'd grown up with
Gerry. A quick letter to him would ease his mind. He could
word his reference so that it did him no harm and me some
good. The second name was the Toronto Bank of Com-
merce, Yonge Street branch. It was years since I'd closed my
account there.

Pardoe put the pad away in a drawer and came to his feet.
He hooked thumbs behind the lapels of his brown tweed
jacket and started walking up and down. I don't know
whether it was the gravity of his voice that lulled me, the
warm, softly-lit room, or the fact that I was still sitting there.
But I listened attentively as he talked with bent head.

"There are certain facts you'll have to accept, Mr. Bain.
Mrs. Straight makes a very credible witness. I could
see you were impressed. That's the danger. The truth
is that she's a highly emotional woman who has undergone a
tragic experience within the last few months. It's left her in a
very disturbed state of mind. This fear, for example. You
were quite right about it. But it's a fear that's completely
unwarranted. The reasons only exist in her mind. You see,
it's her husband she's afraid of." He stopped to make his
point, waiting as if he expected me to say something.

"Some women are," I suggested. "What's so special about
it?"

He ran a hand over smooth white hair, frowning. "I'll tell
you what makes it special. Her husband committed suicide
nearly seven months ago. He did it in a particularly unpleas-
ant way. Blew most of his head off with a twelve-bore shotgun. She still hasn't got over it. That's in spite of the fact
that the last two years of their married life were lived apart.

14

The circumstances are peculiar. Mark Straight was a difficult man to cope with. Eccentric, with an unhealthy interest in the occult. And jealous. Do you know what jealousy can do to a man, Mr. Bain?"

I lit a fresh cigarette, remembering my own cozy theory about jealousy. Any woman I was interested in who preferred someone else was crazy. It was no more *than* a theory. Kirstie gave me no trouble and I'd never been interested in anyone else.

"I've heard tell," I answered.

He shook his head slowly. "I don't suppose you've heard anything quite like this. Straight was obsessed with the idea that his wife had been betraying him since the day of their marriage. A cruel idea and totally false. But he made her life hell because of it."

"Why did she stay with him?" I asked bluntly. "For his money?"

He walked across to a cupboard by the safe. He looked back as he opened it, his voice dry.

"I don't think you *are* a judge of character. Why *do* women do these things? I've been practicing law for thirty-five years and I still don't know the answer. He left a note for the coroner, blaming Mrs. Straight for his suicide. Again, cruel and totally false. It shocked her deeply. She saw it as a deliberate and planned attack on her. The tragedy is that she still thinks she has something to fear from him. Her mind turns commonplace happenings into something sinister."

"Like what?"

He pulled a double-barreled shotgun out of the cupboard.

"Threats from the grave," he said distinctly. He hefted the gun in his hand. "The firm has acted for the family for two generations, my father before me. You could say that I was Mark Straight's friend — as much as he allowed anyone to be a friend. I had to be the one to find him. This gun was returned to me by the police after the inquest. I was the executor. It's been here ever since, a memento, I suppose you might call it, to a man whose worst enemy was himself."

He locked the gun away in the cupboard and returned to his desk. He sat quietly for a minute, toying with his spectacles.

"You're probably wondering why I'm telling you all this?" he asked suddenly.

He was way off the mark. What I was doing was multiplying forty by twelve. The product was nearly five hundred pounds. The thought made me respectful.

"All *I'm* concerned with, Mr. Pardoe, is what you want from me."

He pushed a cuticle back with the end of a paper knife. "That's not difficult. You're expected to be loyal to the people who have Mrs. Straight's well-being at heart. The rest is unimportant."

A buzzer sounded on his desk. He leaned toward the intercom box, his face impatient at the interruption.

I waited until he had finished. "Fair enough. Then figuratively speaking, I'm supposed to hold her hand, is that it?"

He massaged his chin thoughtfully. "You're supposed to do as you're told, Mr. Bain," he said finally. "This is Mrs. Straight's idea from start to finish. I'll be frank with you. I disapprove strongly but there's nothing I can do about it. I'm not paying your salary. For that matter, nor is she."

16

It seemed as though someone had slipped a handful of ice cubes down my neck.

"Then who is?" I asked.

"Her brother-in-law," Pardoe answered. "Mark Straight was a wealthy man when they married but he was foolish with money. He gave away large sums to charlatans — esoteric organizations run by people who were no better than confidence-tricksters. Practically speaking, all he left Jessica is the house she lives in and her jewelry. There was no insurance, of course."

The reference to con-men had pulled me up short. I did my best to sound nonchalant.

"Then surely *he* takes her seriously? I mean if he's paying for all this?"

Pardoe wiped the corners of his mouth with a silk handkerchief.

"I'm not sure *what* he thinks, Mr. Bain. I can only tell you that his sister-in-law is a subject of deep concern to him. John Straight's a man of principle. He has supplemented Mrs. Straight's income ever since his brother's death. You'll meet him tomorrow. I've no idea what his instructions are going to be. He'll tell you that himself."

The answer reassured me. The five hundred pounds were back in my pocket.

"Where does Mrs. Straight live?" I asked idly.

He used three matches to light a cigar. "Kingston Hill," he said between puffs. "You'd better make whatever arrangements are necessary. I'd like you here at half past ten in the morning, ready to move in. Is there anything else you want to know before you go?"

I decided to push my luck. "There'll be bills to pay if I'm

17

going to be away for three months. The truth is that I don't have that sort of money at the moment."

He took the cigar from his mouth, spoke through the intercom. A secretary appeared. He took the envelope she gave him, waiting until she was gone before opening it. He counted out eight 5-pound notes and shoved them across the desk.

"We'll call this an advance against your first month's salary. And in spite of anything I said, don't think that I begrudge it. Put your signature here."

A well-manicured nail marked the spot on the receipt form. I scribbled my name and put the money in my pocket. Pardoe smiled at me in friendly fashion.

"Don't worry about it. I know something about the ups and downs of life, Mr. Bain."

I came to my feet, feeling as though I'd just robbed an alms box. It would have been easier if he'd spared me the sympathy. I collected my coat and went through to the reception office. The girl's voice stopped me in the doorway.

"Do you have a telephone number, Mr. Bain?"

She uncrossed her legs, revealing red boy-bafflers. Her voice suggested a hint of patronage.

I gave her my number. "It won't do you any good after tomorrow."

She showed small teeth, white and sharp like a cat's. "It's Mr. Pardoe who wants it, not me."

It was still raining outside. I took a cab back to Chelsea, paying it off in front of the Public Library. Almost six o'clock. Kirstie was rarely home before half past. I went upstairs to the Reference Room. It was empty save for a bearded and turbaned Sikh doing his homework and an elderly man fighting a nervous cough. I carried the armful of books to a table. *Who's Who. The Directory of Directors. The Voter's List* for the Borough of Kingston. Half an hour's study gave me more facts about the Straight family than I had hoped for. Mark and John were the only children of the late Hammond Straight, founder of the Kowloon Shipping Line. The company had gone public in 1954. Both sons had been educated at Eton. Mark had been thirty-nine when he died. John was a couple of years younger and unmarried. I found Jessica Straight's name in the voting list. Inevitably, the house was called *Kowloon*. Two occupants were listed at the time of the last register in 1966. Jessica Sara Straight and Martha Moody.

I put the books back on the shelves and went downstairs. It was seven o'clock by the time I turned into Kirstie's apartment block, a building behind Chelsea Post Office. Her flat was on the second floor. I rang the doorbell, setting myself in a position of casual triumph. She reached up, standing on the tips of her stockinged feet to kiss me. She wriggled herself free, cocked her head to one side, and inspected me. Her new hairstyle was my own idea, a low fringe over her hazel eyes. Two sweeps of dark chestnut framed a tilted nose and wide, determined mouth. She was wearing a plum-colored velvet skirt and a white silk blouse.

I hung my hat and coat in the small hallway. She pushed me into the sitting room and swung me round. I still remembered the flat as it had been when the agent showed us round. Three bare rooms, bleak in the spring sunshine. Four years had transformed the place. She'd ripped off the flowered wallpaper, junked all the kitchen fixtures and tiled the bathroom in pink. Cream curtains matched the walls in each room. The Danish-designed furniture wouldn't have been my choice but it was easy on the eye and comfortable. The Dufy print I'd given her hung over the fireplace — a misty impression of horses going to post. One of these days I was supposed to be moving in here.

She looked me up and down again, her eyes mocking. "Well, now, this *is* a surprise! Don't tell me you've spent the day in the Victoria-and-Albert Museum. Such elegance. Words fail me!"

I lowered myself into a chair. "Why don't you come off it! When did words ever fail *you?* You are looking at a man in gainful employment, Kirstie. Forty pounds a week, all found, with a guarantee of three months."

She sat down very slowly, her eyes on my face. "You're a liar," she said flatly.

I took a deep breath. I hadn't been kidding myself. This wasn't going to be easy. I shook a cigarette from the pack and lit it carefully.

"I'm *not* lying, darling. I've found a job starting as of ten-thirty tomorrow morning. Do you want to hear the rest of it or not?"

She pulled her legs up under her, toes twitching and curling as she continued to watch me narrowly.

"A job doing what? Who with?"

"A Mrs. Jessica Straight." I pointed out at the kitchen. "If there's anything cooking, you'd better turn it off. This might take time."

"We've got all night," she said evenly. "And nothing *is* cooking. You're having Chinese food out of a can. Who is Jessica Straight?"

There is only one way to deal with Kirstie — to tell her the truth. But there's a snag. If the truth isn't exactly what she wants to hear, it can be around a long while before it's accepted. We'd first met at an exhibition billed as the "Real-Tennis Championship of England." The match was staged before forty people on an enclosed court in an Elizabethan manor house. Kirstie had come with a party. My presence was strictly professional. My interest was in a house a couple of miles across the parkland. A lady high on my list of prospects had rented it for the season. Mrs. Hartrup was an American widow with a collection of jewelry that I'd catalogued from close observation.

I'd seen Kirstie's party break up, after a gin-fired argument. I'd given her a lift back to London. Something sparked between us. We began seeing a lot of one another. As soon as I was sure that the interest was mutual, I told her about my past. I said nothing about my present. A couple of months later, her father rectified the omission. He'd hired private detectives to do some research on me. I confirmed his worst suspicions by getting myself arrested the following January.

I climbed out of the chair and opened the bar cupboard. She shook her head as I held up the whisky bottle. I poured myself a stiff jolt and added water. It was somehow easier to talk to her, standing.

"Jessica Straight is a widow in need of care and protection. She and her lawyer have decided that I'm the guy to supply them."

I told her about the advertisement in the *Telegraph*, the interview at King's Bench Walk. She just sat there, twiddling her toes, for once letting me finish without interruption. Suddenly she swung her hair back.

"If you say 'I swear it's the truth' just once more, I'll scream. Why *should* a respectable lawyer choose you of all people to take care of some neurotic old bag? Does he know you've been in prison?"

I put my glass down with a crash. "No, he doesn't! And just for the sake of the record, Jessica Straight's an elegant, attractive woman of thirty-five. But don't let that worry you."

"I see," she said slowly. "You must be feeling very proud of yourself."

I shifted my shoulders, determined to give as good as I got for once.

"After eleven months of getting the bum's rush every time I beat my breast and bawled *mea culpa*, I told a lie for once and got myself a job. What's that supposed to make me, a leper?"

She picked at a seam in her skirt, avoiding my hostile look. "You still won't believe that people — *real* people, anyway — aren't interested in what you were, only in what you are."

I shook a finger at her. "These real people you talk about, where are they — Boy Scout Headquarters? What about your father, is *he* one of them?"

Her reaction was swift and combative. "Suppose we leave my father out of it. He doesn't owe you a living any more than the others do!"

"Now," I said, nodding. "*Now* we finally made it! Nobody owes me a living. Don't I have the right to earn one? What do they want from me first, public purification?"

She stared hard at me. "Value, that's what they want. And don't bother listing your accomplishments. I'd sooner not think about most of them. You're nearly thirty-six. Two years' university, no degree. What else do you have to offer — we'll forget the Tangier episode. The name of the place alone is enough to put most people off."

I held my hand up. "Would you mind smiling when you say things like that? You make it sound like drug-running, white-slave traffic! I'd have you know that *La Compagnie Marocaine Minière et Industrielle* was a legitimate enterprise, overworked and under-capitalized."

She beat her palms together softly. "End of commercial, organ-sting and out! And it was doomed to go bankrupt. You don't have any specialized training. Not the kind we'll talk about. All right — fluent French and German. If you'd stayed with the travel bureau, you could have used them."

"I could have used them in Soho," I answered. "Wearing false whiskers and a rented cossack suit, shilling for the tourist traps."

She set her face in an expression of exasperation. "I give up! It's impossible to have a serious discussion with you. I suppose you gave false references, too," she added as an afterthought.

"You suppose wrong," I answered. The discussion was unfair, unrealistic, and useless. "For Crissakes, smile, Kirstie. You look like an indignant Pekingese. I love you. If it matters to you that much, I'll forget the whole thing."

She was on her feet instantly, generous as always in victory. "I love you as well, Macbeth Bain. Too much to stop you now. You'd blame me, every time you remembered."

There were times when that small head was too wise for me. "Tell me something," I challenged. "Why is it always

23

that you're the one who wants to change me. Why isn't it ever the other way round?"

She looked at me from under her fringe. "I'll let you answer that question. Pour yourself another drink and tell me about the fascinating Mrs. Straight."

All Kirstie had done was change the field of battle. "I didn't say she was fascinating," I reminded her. "I said she was frightened."

She dropped a mock curtsy. "Then I apologize. Frightened and elegant. I'm not surprised that her lawyer thinks something's wrong with her. The whole family sounds peculiar. And you're going to move into this poor creature's house and give her sympathy and understanding. Charming."

I yawned, shaking my head at her. "Always the cheerful little helpmate. You don't give up easily, do you? I thought all this had been decided."

"It has," she snapped. "Now if you'll open the wine, I'll serve the food."

I followed her out to the kitchen. There was a bowl of freesias on the table. The smell reminded me of my mother. At that, so did Kirstie in her present mood. We ate chow-mein by candlelight.

Dinner over, we watched television with the lights out. Rain beat softly against the windows. We sat close together on the sofa. The images on the screen meant nothing to me. I was busy parlaying five hundred pounds into an entirely different kind of dreamworld. I lifted her head from my lap and switched the set off. My shoes and tie were on the floor. I padded over to the dresser for my cigarettes. She watched me from the sofa, raising herself lazily as I spoke.

"Listen to this, Kirstie. A Crime Consultant Bureau for

24

burglary-prone celebrities. Set a thief to catch a thief. With me on their side, the insurance companies could reduce their premiums by ten percent."

She swung her feet to the ground. "You're like a small boy with a chemistry set, my darling. One spark and you've discovered electricity. What happens if someone robs your clients?"

I gave the problem the thought it deserved. "You missed the point. My clients wouldn't *be* robbed. I know too many answers."

She switched the lights on and shook up the cushions. "I wonder," she said in a small tired voice.

I took my empty wine glass out to the kitchen. She had my shoes in her hand when I came back. I shook my head at her.

"I just don't believe it. You wouldn't turn a dog out on a night like this."

She narrowed her eyes menacingly. "An elegant, attractive woman! Well, let me tell you something, Macbeth Bain. If you as much as look at her, I'll know. Now, for God's sake, don't make any noise. I have enough trouble with the neighbors as it is." She vanished into the bathroom.

Her bedroom was white and gold. The picture of me on the dressing table was four years old. There'd been no gray hairs over the ears then. I was laughing. For some reason, Kirstie liked it. The *real* Macbeth, she said — whatever that meant. I switched on the electric blanket and crawled between the sheets. It was some time before the bathroom door opened on the fragrance of *L'air du Temps*. Then the warmth of her body was joined to mine. There had only been one woman for me — ever. I wouldn't have cared if the world had stopped.

Tuesday

THE RADIO was playing next door. Kirstie was lying on her side, fingers curled over her mouth. Her dark hair fanned over the pillow. It was quarter past seven by the traveling clock by the bedside. I ran a bath, used her razor to shave and made tea. I was fully dressed when I carried the cup in to her. I sat down on the end of the bed. She tilted her head warningly at the wall. The radio was loud.

"He can't hear with that racket going on," I said. "Even if he's got his ear glued against the wall. Listen to me, just as soon as I'm settled in, I'll call you — ok?"

She nodded, putting the cup down and holding me tight before releasing me.

"What are you thinking?" she asked suddenly.

The question caught me off guard. I should have known better. She used it often enough. I put my hand under her chin, shaking her head gently.

"That I wouldn't trade you in for another model, not even at eight o'clock in the morning."

She frowned fiercely. "You wouldn't *dare!* My God, is it really as late as that? Don't forget to take slippers and a dressing gown. I'm sure Mrs. Straight runs a perfectly ordered household."

26

I got to my feet, looking down at her. Five-feet-two of nothing and about as easy to fool as a Swiss banker.

"Adversity makes strange bedfellows," I said and reached the door a split second before the pillow was hurled at my head. I let myself out of the flat, making sure that the corridor was empty. The only person I met was the milkman in the lobby. The rain outside had stopped. A cold wind was scattering the leaves across St. Luke's churchyard. I walked north on Sydney Street, and cut through at the back of the hospitals to Elm Park Gardens.

Gribble was coming downstairs as I entered the hall. He caught me before I could reach my own door, a tall man with soft white flesh, a flared overcoat and curly-brimmed bowler. He gave me the benefit of an up-and-down stare. Our dislike was mutual.

"Someone's been putting their rubbish in my bin again," he said petulantly. "Women's stockings and God knows what. It wouldn't be you, I suppose?" His manner made it plain that he really had no doubt. He'd complained about me twice already to the owner's agent. Once about Kirstie's car being parked on the sidewalk. The second time about me burning junk in the garden.

"If the stockings were dirty," I said deliberately, "it was probably your girlfriend." I shut the door on his startled face.

Coming home after spending the night with Kirstie always disenchanted me. I changed into a pair of corduroy slacks, rubber-soled loafers and a sport jacket. I packed a gray suit, some shirts and underclothes, an extra pair of shoes. Long training prompted me to take my passport. I added a manila envelope full of Kirstie's letters and closed my bag. There was no more to do except write a couple of notes, stopping the milk and bread deliveries. I left these on the hall table outside and phoned for a cab.

King's Bench Walk was already lively with gowned and wigged barristers hurrying in all directions. A couple of cars were parked before Pardoe's office. A gray Bentley with Mulliner coachwork. The license plates bore the numbers EP 100. The other car was a brand new Mercedes. A dark coat with a velvet collar was thrown over the back of the driver's seat. I carried my bag into the reception office. The blonde was sitting at the switchboard. She glanced at the clock as the door opened.

"Mr. Pardoe's waiting for you." It was only twenty past ten but she managed to make it sound like *lèse-majesté*. She threw a switch and announced me.

Pardoe was wearing the same brown tweeds, polka-dotted bow tie and a rosebud in his lapel. He came to his feet, thrusting his hand out.

"All prepared, I see. Put your things down anywhere. This is Mr. Straight."

I draped the sheepskin coat over my bag and nodded at the man on my left. His hair was cut to a short brush that stood stiffly from his scalp. He had the same type of spectacles as Pardoe, heavy frames with thick sidepieces. A thin nose and mouth. A dark suit worn with a black tie gave him an appearance of extreme severity. We all sat. Pardoe behind the desk, Straight near enough for me to touch him. He was drumming his fingers on the edge of his chair, contemplating me. I fished a cigarette from the box Pardoe offered. He gave me a light, glancing over his shoulder at Straight.

"I think Mr. Bain knows what to expect. I've briefed him on the circumstances."

Straight's voice belied his appearance. It was soft and regretful.

"Of course. Well, it's an unhappy situation as you'll have seen, Mr. Bain. I regret deeply the need to bring a stranger into what should be entirely a family matter. I'm afraid my sister-in-law left me no choice. You've met her — what was your impression?"

I had an odd feeling that he was challenging the lawyer. The ash glowed on my cigarette. I took a long drag before answering.

"A woman in trouble — a woman who's scared out of her wits."

Straight leant forward, emphasizing the words with a finger. "I'm glad you've been frank, Mr. Bain. I'm having to rely on other people's opinions. You see, Mrs. Straight and I have never met. It was inevitable. I have lived abroad much of the time and my brother tended to isolate her from any company except his own. You'll understand the difficulty. Her well-being is a matter that's very much on my conscience. However there's a limit to what I can do — to what she'll *allow* me to do. I've had to work through Mr. Pardoe and we don't always see eye to eye." He smiled at the lawyer.

It was cutting my own throat but I couldn't resist saying it. "I'd have thought a doctor would have been an obvious solution."

Pardoe was staring at the top of the desk, fiddling with his pencil. It was Straight who answered.

"There isn't a chance of it. My sister-in-law is a very determined woman, you'll find. Any suggestion of that sort could only aggravate matters. There's something else, Mr. Bain. She mistrusts everything that reminds her of my brother. No, she's the one who has taken this decision. In spite of everything, I feel it's my duty to try to help her."

Pardoe swung his chair round, fingertips pressed together. "I think we'd better discuss the question of scandal while we're about it."

Straight shrugged. "My brother's suicide — the notoriety and unpleasantness that went with it — came as a shock to me, Mr. Bain. I've always tried to lead a contemplative sort of life. Nevertheless, it's not myself I'm concerned with at the moment. Any fresh scandal would ruin her completely."

I dribbled a stream of smoke from my nostrils. "I can see that."

He gave me a card. "Here's my telephone number. Don't hesitate to use it if necessary. Mr. Pardoe will be your point of reference. Let him know how things are going and, by the way, don't as much as mention my name to Mrs. Straight. It can only do more harm than good."

I picked my coat from the floor. "I'll not forget anything you've told me, gentlemen. I'll be in touch."

I took a cab to the top of Kingston Hill. The wind had slackened, even up there. An unbroken ceiling of clouds had dropped low over the distant rooftops. I walked down, following Pardoe's directions. The wide deserted road descended in a steep slope that curved out of sight a couple of hundred yards below. Smoke plumed behind a nearby hedge, acrid with the stink of burning leaves. The scene was almost pastoral. Every means had been used to achieve privacy.

Wall, trees, and shrubbery concealed each house from the road and its neighbor. The only sign of life was a black Labrador watching me from the driveway. It barked dutifully as I neared, its lashing tail an assurance of friendliness. I walked on to a pair of white gates. The name KOWLOON was spelled out on the wall in copper lettering. A hoop of iron secured the gates.

A two-story house built in seventeenth-century style lay behind a curve of asphalt. The front showed rectangular leaded windows, oak timber, and gables over the guttering. Moss and mold mellowed the red brickwork. There was a porch at the head of the steps, a wrought iron lantern over the nail-studded door. I pressed the bell. Chimes sounded inside. The door opened abruptly. A middle-aged woman in a maid's uniform peered out. She had a thin suspicious face and red carroty hair scraped back in a bun.

Her chin lifted a fraction. "Yes?"

I gave her my name. "Mrs. Straight's expecting me," I added.

The announcement didn't appear to enthrall her. But she backed off, letting me into a carpeted hall. A coal fire was burning in a large grate. Something else was burning — joss-sticks. A couple of church chairs with tooled-leather backs stood each side of the fireplace. Mrs. Straight's voice sounded somewhere beyond the head of the staircase facing me.

"What is it, Martha?"

The maid bustled to the foot of the stairs. "Someone for you, ma'am. A Mr. Bain. Where shall I put him?" Her tone suggested a dungeon would be appropriate.

"In the drawing room, Martha," Mrs. Straight called. "I'll be down in a minute."

The maid sniffed and turned a doorhandle. "You can wait in here," she said ungraciously.

The room was at the back of the house. French windows opened onto a leafy lawn spiked with croquet hoops. There were rose bushes outside, still bright with blossom and a fish pond. Blue tits crowded on a bird platform, pecking at bags of peanuts. Beyond the yew hedge that skirted the garden was a clear view of Coombe Wood. I took my coat off and looked round. The decoration had been planned with taste and thought. There were four vigorous paintings of horses in action, the colors bright against linen-textured wallpaper. The chairs were elegant. There were some pieces of bronze and a French *escritoire*. An enormous chintz-covered sofa straddled the thick golden carpet. The door was open at the far end of the room. I walked over and peeped through. A fire was burning in front of a low table littered with newspapers and magazines. The joss-stick I'd smelled smoldered beside a bowl of roses. One wall was completely covered with books. There was a desk and an oil painting of Mrs. Straight. The artist had portrayed her against a dark blue background. She was smiling at a point somewhere above my shoulder, her hands holding a sheaf of flowers. She couldn't have been more than eighteen.

I moved away quickly as I heard her voice in the hall. The drawing room door opened. She was wearing tan stretch slacks, low shoes, and a cashmere sweater. A hoop of brown velvet secured her ash-blond hair behind her ears. She looked at the empty fireplace, frowning.

"I'd completely forgotten — I'm sorry. Let's go into the study."

She pushed a chintz-wrapped armchair at me and sat down, fitting a cigarette into her long holder. I gave her a light. She inhaled deeply as though she'd been waiting for it a long time.

"I should have warned you about Martha. She's been with me for eleven years. I'm afraid it shows."

I smiled. "I've survived worse welcomes."

A network of fine lines gathered near her cheekbones. "She's like that with everyone. She thinks she's protecting me. It's something you'll have to get used to. It'll only be during the day. She won't be sleeping in the house while you're here."

"No," I said noncommittally. "You have a very pleasant house, Mrs. Straight."

Her voice was deliberate. "We're grown-up people. You don't have to make polite conversation. If I didn't trust you, you wouldn't be here. Surely that's obvious."

Her violet eyes were steady and frank. I was no psychiatrist but it was difficult to believe that the brain behind them wasn't as rational as mine.

"If I hadn't understood that," I said quietly, "I wouldn't be here, either."

"Good. Then we understand one another." Her smile came and went. "You'd like to see your room."

She led the way into the hall. Upstairs was a long corridor, bright with bowls of begonias. At the back of my mind I suppose I'd expected to find a sort of Frankenstein manor house, dripping in mist. There was something incongruous about Aldin prints, a pair of treed riding boots standing outside a door, her own sureness of manner. The room she opened for me overlooked the front of the house. There were twin beds with padded headboards, a blue carpet and curtains, a large closet. Someone had put fruit and cigarettes on the table between the beds. She showed me the adjoining bathroom.

"I think you'll find all you want. You're completely self-contained here. My room's at the other end of the corridor." I saw the expression change in her eyes. It was the look of someone who remembers and is afraid. She lifted a hand to the back of her hair. "I have to go out. Lunch is at one o'clock. Tell Martha what you need. She'll be going about four. I should be back by five. You can look round the house and tell me what you think."

I threw my bag on the nearest bed and unfastened it. She was still standing in the doorway. I put Kirstie's picture on the dressing table, facing the bed.

"What am I supposed to be looking for?" I asked casually.

She flicked the light switch up and down uncertainly. "You said it was a pleasant house. You're wrong. It used to be. Not any more. It's *evil*." Her mouth was trembling.

I'm always unsure, confronted with a woman on the verge of tears. Especially tears for a reason unknown to me. I started unpacking my bag. When I turned round she was smiling.

"You're not a prisoner, Mr. Bain. I'll leave a key for you downstairs. But I would be glad if you're here when I get back." A few minutes later I heard a car. I went to the window. She was backing a blue Mini-Cooper out of the garage. She drove off, leaving the gates open. I finished my unpacking and went downstairs. A green baize door off the hall led to the kitchen. I went into the drawing room and out through

the French windows. I walked aimlessly in the garden, trying
to think.

A speckled thrush was hacking at a coconut shell on the
bird platform. The simple peace of the scene heightened the
problem of Mrs. Straight. One thing was sure. I couldn't be
of help till she told me what was troubling her. A gong
sounded inside. I went back into the house. Lunch was
served in the study. I worked my way through cold cuts and
salad, ducking the caramel flan. My one attempt to break
the maid down fell flat on its face. There were wines and
spirits in the house, she said. If I wanted beer, I could fetch
it myself. The meal was over. I called Kirstie at the agency.
I hadn't the nerve to tell her that I'd be alone in the house
with Mrs. Straight at night. Luckily she was busy. I promised I'd phone later. It was quiet and warm in the study.
I must have dozed off, sitting in the armchair.

It was half past four when I woke up. The house was
dark and empty. Twenty minutes later, I heard the roar of
the Mini returning. Jessica Straight was hurrying up the steps,
pulling a chiffon scarf from her head. I went to meet her.
We stood in the hall for a second, the fire crackling at our
backs. She tossed a couple of packages on a chair and bolted
the front door. She switched the lights on, glancing up
the staircase. She made a face, shivering slightly.

"I *hate* this time of the day. I wish Martha would remember to draw the curtains before she goes. Did anyone telephone?"

"I wouldn't know," I admitted. "I slept. But I've discovered one thing about this house."

She seemed to make a habit of staring into corners then

turning her head quickly, as if expecting to surprise someone or something.

"What?"

I grinned from the study doorway. "It's built like a fortress. Burglar-proof bolts on all the windows. Chubb locks on the outside doors. Impregnable."

She let her breath go. "My husband had that done some years ago. I'll make some tea. You must be dying of thirst."

She brought the tray into the study. I had the feeling, watching her clear the table, that I knew why she spent so much time in this room. A couple of steps took her either into the drawing room or the hall. The windows were set at right angles, giving a view of the front of the house and the back. She pulled the curtains and poured orange-scented tea from a willow-pattern pot. She gave me a cup and saucer.

"Do you believe in the supernatural, Mr. Bain?"

The book-lined room and bright fire combined in a memory that was twenty-six years old and three thousand miles away. My grandfather's voice, firm with the certainty of inner conviction: *The hell with your philosophers, Macbeth. God's promise of a hereafter is something they'll have to learn the hard way.* It was a promise still unproven, as far as I was concerned. I put my cup down on a pile of magazines.

"If you mean what I think you mean, no."

She stood in front of the fire, her hands behind her back. "That's what I expected you to say. How much did Pardoe tell you about my husband?"

I raised the lid of a silver cigarette box. The inscription inside was dated March 1949. *Jessica Sara Powell — Burford Hunter Trials.* I spaced the words between inhalations.

"Not much really. A difficult man to live with — jealous, that sort of thing."

"Typical," she said. She sat down in the other armchair, dragging it towards me. I saw now why she'd kept her hands behind her. They were trembling. "There's more than that, Mr. Bain. A great deal more. If you're going to be able to help me, you've got to know what sort of man he really was. No matter what people say I married for love. The day after the wedding I realized that I'd married a complete stranger. Have you ever seen jealousy at work?"

"I don't think so," I said. "I don't know. I suppose it's a part of love, isn't it? *I'm* not an expert on the subject."

Her cup clattered down on the tray. "I am. Nobody really knew my husband except me. He put on a show that convinced everyone. People talked about his kindness to me, his thoughtfulness. Nobody saw the change as soon as we were alone. The length he'd go to humiliate me. Can you understand what it means to a woman to be accused of unfaithfulness by the man she loves? Horrible accusations without a vestige of truth in them. He spared nobody. No one was too unlikely. Workmen who came to the house, strangers we met. I no longer had any friends. He'd taken care of that. After eleven years of it, something just snapped and I suddenly saw him as he was — a monster." Her voice broke.

I poured myself some more tea, avoiding looking at her. "All that's over and you're still a very attractive woman. It's the present that counts not the past." Conversations were repeating themselves.

"O *God!*" she said helplessly. The next words were almost spat at me. "Isn't there anything else you can think of?

37

You make me sick, the lot of you! With your stupid suggestions. 'Be patient with her. Humor her!' Don't bother denying it. I can hear Pardoe's voice in everything you say. Isn't it true?"

The violence of her outburst took me by surprise. I looked at her for a good five seconds before replying.

"It's true," I admitted.

She dragged her fingers across her face. "And I'm not making things any easier for you. That's what you mean, isn't it. I'm sorry. I don't know why I had to inflict that on you."

"Why not try me?" I said quietly.

She fitted yet another cigarette into her holder, ice-calm suddenly. Dangerously calm, I thought. The effort it was taking showed in the tenseness of her body.

"All right. When our marriage did finally break up it was my husband who left me, not vice versa. Still playing the part, doing the *decent* thing, you see. Everyone fell for it, including Pardoe. I was left this house. He gave me a fair allowance. Nobody knew of the telephone calls over the last two years — the constant threats."

"What sort of threats?"

She blew smoke toward the chimney, watching the draft suck it in. She shook her head.

"How *can* I explain? It all sounds so innocent. I suppose I'd better tell you that I didn't have a normal childhood. My mother was a Spiritualist, you see. Everything had a special significance — darkness, the tapping of a blind-cord on the window. I used to lie in bed, terrified, waiting for God knows what horror to appear. I grew up with a fear of anything to do with the occult. Mark knew it. Eight years ago he joined a Spiritualist movement."

38

My mind picked its way through the implications. I was a whole lot less sure of myself than I wanted to be.

"How about the threats?" I reminded her.

A clock behind us chimed six. "I'm coming to those," she said. "He pretended to think that I believed in all of it — voices from beyond the grave, manifestations. He'd talk about it quite calmly, watching me from the corner of his eye, smiling. After he left me, he started telephoning. Sometimes once a day, sometimes more. The message was always the same. Dying wasn't permanent. I must never feel lonely. He would always be with me. Then he committed suicide. The note he left for the coroner blamed me for his death. Sometimes I wonder if it isn't true. God knows I hated him enough."

She sat for a while, staring into space. Suddenly she got up and went to a closet under the bookshelves. She pulled out a small record player, turned a switch and lowered the needle. The sound of a church organ swelled in the room. She let the record run briefly and then silenced it.

"That's Handel," she said quietly. "Mark and I used to listen to it when we were first married. There are two telephones in the house. This one and the one upstairs in my bedroom. That's on a separate line. For the last week, someone's been calling me on the upstairs phone. Always about the same time, eleven o'clock, when I'm going to bed. I pick the receiver up and all I hear is this record. Just the beginning of it, then silence." She sat down in the chair again. I looked at her narrowly, trying to square what she'd said with credibility. It was hard to listen to her and disbelieve. I think it was the complete absence of drama that influenced me.

39

"Haven't you told anyone about this?" I asked. "Pardoe or someone?"

She shook her head slowly. "What's the good? I already know what they think. I want to know what *you* think."

It wasn't easy to tell her. My basic feeling was one of sympathy. Behind that was a suspicion that the division between fact and fancy might no longer exist for her.

"The only thing worrying me at the moment is why you had to put an advertisement in a newspaper. Leave Pardoe out of it. Couldn't you have gone to a friend?"

"I *have* no friends," she said stonily.

I don't know what prompted me to say it — the interviews with Pardoe had left me slightly uneasy. An odd sensation — bafflement, maybe, like turning to talk to an old friend and finding a stranger there in his place.

"What about your husband's family?"

Her reaction was exactly as Straight had predicted. "I'd sooner die than ask help from any of them. Can't you understand? I loathe everything that reminds me of him. You've been round the house. There isn't a picture of him — nothing left that belonged to him."

"You kept that record," I reminded her.

She was on her feet in a flash, ripping it from the turntable. She crossed the room deliberately and threw it on the fire. She stood over it till the disc was a curl of stinking ash. She lit another joss-stick, laughing uncertainly.

"What they call 'laying the ghost,' Mr. Bain."

She sat down again primly, using a buffing-board on her long, well-shaped nails. I had another odd feeling. This time that she was putting me on.

40

"Are you telling me the truth, Mrs. Straight?" I said suddenly.

She turned her head, looking at the result of her manicure. She didn't answer.

"What's the matter?" I went on. "Did I say something wrong?"

She laughed in a forced way. "It would be funny if it weren't so desperate. You're trying so hard, aren't you? Let's change the subject. Are you a chess player?"

The switch of manner didn't fool me. I was more certain than ever that she was holding something back.

"I play chess," I admitted. "It's not the same thing."

She gathered the tea things on the tray. "Then it'll give us something to do, won't it?" she said lightly. "I mean, while we're waiting." She smiled and picked the tray up.

I went after her into the hall. The lights were blazing everywhere.

"Waiting for what?" I asked.

She kicked the green baize door open, glancing back over her shoulder.

"The telephone call."

The kitchen made my own look what it was — a slot with a stove. This one was straight out of the Ideal Homes Exhibition. One complete wall of white enamel and aluminum, with enough dials and controls for a jet-liner. Tubular ceiling lights searched every corner of the gleaming floor. She stacked the cups and saucers in a dishwashing machine. A fat marmalade cat unwound itself from a cushion on a chair near the back door. It wreathed towards her, stiff-tailed and purring. She raised the lid of a deep-freeze unit, peering into it uncertainly.

"I'm the worst cook in the world, I'm afraid. We're absolutely at Martha's mercy. She's prepared our dinners for the next four days. You can take your pick from steak-and-kidney pudding, baked ham and pineapple, lamb chops. God knows what this is. It looks like some sort of stew."

The cat was rubbing itself against my leg, shedding its hairs on my trousers. I moved it on gently. Two years in a British jail had left me with a cast iron stomach.

"I'm easy," I said. "I'll eat anything but sheep. I've got a block against it."

She emptied a can of sardines onto a plate and squatted on her haunches, facing me. I could see the tops of her breasts, cupped in a lace-bordered bra. I found myself wondering about the rest of her body. The thought was involuntary and entirely academic. She wasn't for me but it was still a waste of woman. Her eyes met mine. I saw the color rising on her neck.

"What did you eat in the jungle?" she asked suddenly.

You start out with one lie and finish with fifty. I'd never been too good at it, anyway. I must have sat through half a dozen documentaries on the Congo. Hard-nosed mercenaries waving machine guns, raped nuns, mutilated missionaries. As far as I could remember, the staple diet of the military was beer.

"Whatever we found," I said vaguely.

"You must tell me about it." There was a hint of sarcasm in her voice. "We'll eat whenever you're hungry. Eight, eight-thirty?"

I nodded. "Is it all right if I use the phone?"

She pushed the cat nearer the plate of fish. "You know where it is."

Kirstie was home and ready with the second phase of the treatment. It rarely varied. Whenever she was mad at me, she invented other interests. This time it was an advertising party on Godfrey Street — *young* people, she added significantly. The ploy was designed to make me feel ancient. I told her to have fun. She promised she would. I hung up, more or less sure that she'd have cooled off by morning.

We ate in the study, the steak-and-kidney pie with a bottle of Beaujolais. I drank most of the wine. Mrs. Straight's glass was still untouched when we finished dinner. She produced a chessboard from the closet under the bookshelves and cleared the table. She left the hall door open. I set the board and we started our game. The noises of the house registered in my brain. An electric motor in the kitchen, turning itself on and off. Wood settling in the paneling. Her play alternated between a sort of slapdash brilliance and sheer stupidity. Twice she let me off the hook, checkmating me just as I thought myself safe. I rearranged the pieces, a bad loser as always.

"I want my head examined. I should have clobbered you at the start. Who taught you to play?"

She answered abstractedly, looking at the clock ticking away in the corner.

"I taught myself from a book. Your move."

This time I concentrated, finishing the game in ten minutes. She put the set away as if glad it was over. It was twenty to eleven.

"I think I'll go up," she said. The smile was painfully weak.

I stood the iron screen in front of the fire. "Do that. I

won't be long. I'm just going to take a look round. What about the cat?"

She was carrying the glass of wine carefully in both hands. "I've already put him out."

I opened the front door. The wind was on the rise, rustling the branches in the trees. I walked out of the circle of light into the darkness. I'd no idea what I was supposed to be looking for — a second-story man flattened against the wall or the late Mark Straight in his winding-sheet. My rubber-soled shoes made no sound along the passage by the garage. The back of the house was in shadow. I crossed the lawn, stumbling through the croquet hoops. The glow of the fire in the study showed through a chink in the drawn curtains. I made the complete circuit, bolted and locked the front door and turned the hall lights off. The fire there was almost out.

She was standing in her doorway, still fully dressed, when I reached the head of the stairs. I could have used the wine in her hand. I had the taste. I leaned against the banister.

"No chains clanking," I reported. "No bodies in the bushes."

Her expression told me that the sally had failed. "I'll leave my door open. You'll hear the phone ring."

I brushed my teeth and lay on the bed in stockinged feet, staring at Kirstie's picture. There was another one who'd made up her mind about my hostess. *Neurotic old bag* was an uncompromising start. It was Kirstie at her most obstinate and there would be three months of it. I thought vaguely of asking Mrs. Straight to invite Kirstie for a meal. A second's reflection axed the idea. I was in enough trouble with

Kirstie as it was. My watch was on the table beside me. I watched the minutes creep by. Eleven o'clock. Ten past. I switched off the light and tiptoed to the corridor. Her door was still open. I undressed, putting on pajamas for the first time in months. Apparently there was to be no Handel tonight. Just as well. It had been a long day. I was almost asleep when a voice shrieked along the corridor; I kicked out of the bedding and sprinted for her room. I threw a switch, meeting myself in the full-length mirror, wild-eyed and disheveled.

"What the hell's going on?" I shouted.

She was sitting up in bed, pointing at the dressing table, unable to answer. A bottle of scent lay on its side, dripping onto the carpet. I looked round the room mechanically. As I neared the foot of the bed, the cat came out, spitting and clawing. It streaked for the open window. I stood the scent bottle on end. She glanced sideways at the phone, her face as white as the sheet dragged up under it.

"You'd better get some sleep," I said curtly.

She turned her back on me, hiding her head in the bedclothes. I cut the light and went back to my own room, leaving the door ajar. It seemed only seconds and I was in a dream where Kirstie smiled at me across a room full of people. But just as I reached her, she changed to Jessica Straight offering me a chessboard.

Wednesday

HABIT AWAKENED ME early. Morning was flaring in the windows. It was still and quiet outside. There was no wind. Frost glistened on the grass and tarmac. I was halfway through shaving when I heard a gate open and shut. Martha hurried in, turning up the path by the side of the garage. I finished dressing and made my bed. Mrs. Straight's door was shut tight. I went downstairs. The fires had been cleaned and relit. I shoved the door leading to the kitchen. Martha was at the stove, a nylon work apron over her uniform. The cat must have followed her in. It was lying on its cushion, curled like a ginger slug. I said good morning tentatively.

She kept her back to me. "Tea or coffee?" she snapped.

I walked over and inspected the tray she had laid. Toast, butter, and orange juice.

"Tea, please. This looks terrific. You must be a mind reader."

She covered a small pot with a quilted cozy. "That's as may be," she said darkly. "Only it's not your tray and I'll thank you not to smoke in my kitchen."

I dropped the butt into a garbage pail. "Look, Martha.

46

I'm going to be around for a while. It'll make things easier for us both if you'll accept that."

She rolled her sleeves up, exposing stringy freckled forearms. Bright blue eyes under ratty hair stared back at me. Certainly she wasn't a man. But that was about as feminine as she could be.

"I've been with her eleven years, Mister," she said. "And there's them as had better remember it."

She lifted the tray and bustled through the baize door, leaving it swinging in my face. I lifted the cat by the scruff and deposited it outside the kitchen door. I'd have done the same to the maid, gladly. I called Kirstie, catching her just out of the bath. It seemed that she'd skipped the party after all. She hoped I'd had a pleasant evening. I gave her an accurate description of it, down to the midnight dash along the corridor. Her voice was sugar-coated.

"In your pajamas, how sweet! I can't wait for the next installment, darling, but it's a quarter to nine. I have to run."

I hung up and ate my breakfast. The morning crept on. Mail was delivered, the newspapers. I went outside and found a croquet mallet in the gardenhouse. I started slamming a ball across the lawn, wondering when Kirstie was going to grow up. It was after eleven when Jessica Straight came through the French windows. She was wearing the same slacks and sweater, her ash hair dragged back in the Alice-band. I stood the mallet against a tree and walked over to her.

"I'm getting the direction. It's the hoops. They're too small."

Her eyes looked tired and she was pale. She moved a hand wearily.

"I'm sorry. That wasn't a very good start, was it?"

I glanced up, catching Martha's face at the window. It vanished immediately. I shrugged. It was her production not mine.

"At least we weren't disturbed by music."

"Please don't be cruel," she said quietly. "You were right last night. I *haven't* told you everything. Come inside and I will."

I wiped my feet carefully and followed her into the study. She shut both the doors and lifted her portrait from the wall. A small safe was concealed behind it. She unlocked her desk, taking out a small key. I watched her use it on the safe, incredulous that people like this never learned. Burglar-conscious to the point of installing a safe, they left the key under a pile of stockings in the top right-hand drawer of the dressing table — or like this, in a hiding place that a child could crack with a wood chisel. The bottom shelf of the safe was loaded with jewel cases. She chose one and put it on the table.

"Open it, please."

I lifted the lid. Inside was a gold pendant on a chain. The pendant was made in the form of a hand. The fingers were articulate and moved when the chain was swung. The effect was macabre.

Her voice was barely audible. "That came through the post two weeks ago. It would have been my twelfth wedding anniversary."

I put the pendant down, scrutinizing her closely. "Are you being serious?"

Her violet eyes were pleading. "I threw the wrapping paper away but the parcel was posted in London. There was no card, no message. The address was typewritten."

The silk lining of the jewel case bore no maker's name. I had a definite feeling of uneasiness.

"And you're telling me that you've never seen this thing before?"

"I've never seen it before in my life," she answered deliberately.

I let the lid drop. Something in her face convinced me that she wasn't lying.

"You still don't believe me, do you," she said sadly. "I can imagine what's in your mind. Why didn't I go to Pardoc? I've already told you why. I'm not a fool, Mr. Bain, I know what he thinks. I'm *not* mentally unbalanced. But I will be unless someone realizes what's happening to me."

"All right, we'll start over again," I said. "Somebody's trying to scare you. Who do you think it is?"

Her answer was barely audible. "I don't know."

"Well, *think!*" I ordered. "You must have some sort of idea."

She stood there, looking at me in silence, tears starting to well in her eyes.

"Then we'll have to find out." I put the pendant in my pocket. "I'll take this with me. Can I borrow your car?"

She unclasped her hands. "Where are you going?"

"Out," I said shortly. "I'll be back after lunch. You'd better lock your safe."

I hung the portrait back on the wall for her, watching her put the key back in the desk.

"You just got yourself a believer," I said.

49

Her face came alive, the look of a girl who's told that she's beautiful.

"The keys are in the car. Will you be long?"

"No longer than I can help." I grabbed my coat from the hall and went out to the garage. The souped-up motor caught at the first turn of the ignition key. I revved it to a high-pitched whine, trying the gears. I left the garage in a series of jerks. I looked in the rear-view mirror as I stopped at the gate. She was standing at the study window.

It was past noon when I reached Hatton Garden. I parked on a side street and walked down past the blank fronts of the wholesale jewelry offices. The street was crowded with brokers, their pockets filled with unset stones wrapped in tissue paper. A prowl car crept by, the cops sitting in front scanning the faces of the people on the sidewalks. I turned into a doorway. Maybe it was my fancy but nothing seemed to have changed in three years. There were still sacks of leather trimmings propped outside the workshop of the Margolis Bag Company. The glass door across the lobby was still padlocked. As long as I'd known the building, HongKong Novelties had never been open for business. The same smell of *lockshen* pudding wafted up from the sandwich bar below.

I climbed up dirty uncarpeted stairs to the second story. A card was pinned on the door facing me. *S. Riffkind, Dealer in Fine Stones.* Scrawled across the card was the message "Back at two." The same hand had added a penciled afterthought. "God willing." I made my way down to the basement. The air was blue with cigarette smoke, the marble-topped tables crowded with gesticulating men. It was hard to detect a word of English in the polyglot babble. A poker-faced Span-

50

iard in a white coat was relaying orders to the counterhand.

"One salt beef on rye. One bean-and-barley soup. Glass water, please."

To an outsider, the place must have looked like a cross between an immigration shed and a B'nai B'rith smoker. The fact was that a fair percentage of the city's diamond trading took place over glasses of lemon tea and *gefüllte fisch*.

Riffkind was sitting in his usual place, a table at the far end of the room near the counter. His coat, hat, and briefcase were spread over the empty chairs. His swarthy face split in an enormous grin as he spotted me. He was built like a bear, with flat black hair and great pads of flesh that held his mouth in an expression of wonder. He cleared a chair for me, wagging his head.

"So look who's here! You want soup and *beigels* — cold salmon, they got. It'll be my pleasure."

A ten-carat brilliant flashed on his hand as he waved theatrically. I sat down next to him.

"I'll take a tea and a plate of salt beef."

He gave the order, his eyes considering me shrewdly. "You been out a long time," he said suddenly. "So why you don't come to see your old friends?"

I jammed the spoon against the slice of lemon, squeezing the juice into the hot brew. Riffkind had limped into the country thirty years ago, carrying a cardboard suitcase and a jeweler's glass. Over the period between, he'd acquired a fifteen-room house in Hampstead, a wife and three sons as big as he was. He was what the fraternity called a safe buyer. When he was sure of the seller, he dealt in hot jewelry, paid cash, and kept his mouth shut.

51

I forked a mouthful of salt beef. "I turned legitimate, Sam. You know, working for a living. I have to watch the company I keep. People expect it."

He finished his sandwich and rapped himself sharply in the region of the chest. He swallowed a pastille.

"Heartburn," he apologized. "So what do you do now, my boy?"

"I open my veins and bleed a little," I answered.

"Na, was!" he said shaking his head again. "*Eat*," he urged. "You got thinner." He used a toothpick, shielding his mouth in genteel fashion. He watched as I finished the meat.

I pushed the plate away. "I brought something with me, Sam," I said softly.

He rose without a word, clicking his fingers for the bill. I followed him out. The stairs groaned under his weight. He opened his office, blowing hard. The curtains were permanently drawn. There were two chairs, a desk with a pair of jeweler's scales. The small room was stuffy with the fumes from a kerosene heater. A framed certificate of naturalization hung on the wall. He thudded into the seat behind the desk, holding out a hand as I produced the suede box. He opened it slowly, as if he expected to see something live inside. He pushed it back as soon as he saw the contents.

"You need a few quid, Mac. I give it for old times sake. But Fagin, I'm not."

I shoved the box back across the desk. "Just take a look at it, Sam," I urged.

His crumpled face was almost shocked. "A good boy like you — chancing his arm for bits of gold. *Dreck!*" He made it sound as though I'd committed sacrilege.

"*Look* at it, goddammit," I said angrily. "I'm not trying to sell you something. I want to know where it came from."

It was a while before he saw that I was serious. He whipped a loupe into his right eye, holding the pendant near his nose as if smelling it. He caught his glass in his palm.

"French or Italian, handmade. Twenty-two carat. Fifty quid in the trade."

He closed the box and returned it to me. "So, retired," he said disbelieving. "Things ain't the same no more. Diamonds is what they want, boy. No pearls, no colored stones."

I refused the cigar he offered. "You don't say! I walk in here with a fist full of emeralds and you tell me I'm wasting your time. That'll be the day, Sam."

He unbuttoned his overcoat and scratched, considering me for a while.

"Why lie to me?" he asked. "We're old friends. I'm going to tell you something, boy. You're an angel from God. You know why. There's a crook downstairs, a no-good *schnorrer* walking about with eight hundred quid, my money. My own wife's brother! Five nights a week he puts his stock in the vaults." He paused, waiting to see the effect of his news.

It was an odd feeling, knowing what was coming. It was the first time Riffkind had ever set a job up for me.

"So do you," I reminded him. A startled look crept over his face. I continued. "I used to see you. Somebody'll belt you over the head one of these nights."

His hand crept involuntarily toward his briefcase. He winked unconvincingly. "I don't do it no more. Listen to me, Mac. This *gonef* does a round every Saturday morning.

Even the Sabbath he don't keep. He goes round North London — good trade, I'll give the bastard that. But here's the secret. He don't trust nobody. So what happens. I'll tell you. Mr. Garber carries a few pieces in with him. The rest he leaves in the car. Under the seat. You can get keys. I give the times and places. Ten grand, Mac, my own dear life. And what do I want out of it? Nothing! He takes his big nose to the police. 'Sorry, Mr. Garber,' they say. 'Someone must have followed you. We'll be in touch.' He ain't even insured."

I put the box away in the pocket of my coat. "It's not for me, Sam. Thanks all the same. I meant to tell you. I'm starting an advisory service in a couple of months. For people like your brother-in-law. You want to do business, I'll give you a discount."

I left him shaking his head as if he'd seen a ghost. As I turned the corner where I'd parked, I realized that someone was sitting in the Mini. I could see the back of a man's head. I crossed the street and walked down till I came abreast of the car. I recognized the occupant instantly. John Rowlands, otherwise Jack the Rat, the most industrious police informer in the business. Nobody ever told him anything but he had a needle-nose for reconstructing villainy. He was an all-around swell who worked a little blackmail on the side when finking was slow. His protection had slipped the previous year. He'd found himself doing a six months' sentence in Winchester Prison. He lodged two cells away from mine. I'd as soon have seen a cobra in the car as Rowlands.

He saw me in the rear-view mirror and started rolling the window down. Scars slashed his cheeks from the corners of his eyes to his mouth. Rumor had it that his own brother had gone at him a razor in each hand. Certainly his body held more stitches than a sampler. He'd hoed a tough row in jail. I'd never even spoken to him. He pushed his hat back as I opened the door.

"I been waiting for you, Canada."

"Out," I said curtly.

He sat where he was. The lapels of his camel hair coat were stained with either blood or ketchup.

"Things ain't too good, Canada," he said softly.

I looked at him unmoved. "They'll be a hell of a lot worse if you don't get your arse out of this car."

He gave me a National Health Service smile, showing teeth that looked as if they'd been carved out of toothbrush handles.

"That ain't nice," he reproved. "You and me used to be pals."

I almost gagged on the thought. I leaned across smelling the beer on his breath, and unlocked the door on his side.

"Beat it."

"Riffkind," he said stealthily. "Well, good luck to you. I like to see old mates come good again. You got me all wrong, Canada. I don't work for the law no more. They give me the belt."

I realized that he must have seen me arrive, followed me to the café and whipped back to the parked Mini. The squad car could be circling the block again at any minute. The last thing I wanted was to be found sitting next to Rowlands. And he knew it. I made a pretense of searching my pockets and dropped a pound note in his lap.

"That's all there is. Now hit the road."

He picked the note up, folded it lengthwise and started whistling through it.

"You and me's got a little business to discuss," he said finally. "But I ain't in no hurry."

I jerked the door open. "I am. *Move.*"

He sat there shaking his head and then got out reluctantly. He leaned back through the open window.

"I'll give you a ring tonight, mate. And don't worry about me coming out to Kingston. The air'll do me lungs good."

He grinned and was lost in the crowd before I could grab him. My first thought was the glove compartment. The driving license and insurance certificate were still there. I opened them both. Mrs. Straight's name and address was on each document. The damage was done.

I'd been out of jail for nearly a year, the only reminder of the past an occasional name in a crime report. Now suddenly it was all very fresh in my mind. Riffkind, the squad car, the sinister figure in the dirty camel hair coat.

I maneuvered the Mini from the curb and got out of there as fast as I could. Kingston Hill was a pattern of suburban serenity. Children were kicking through the carefully-piled leaves on the pavements. A delivery man was whistling up a driveway. The smell of burning leaves was in the autumnal air. I put the car away and opened the front door with the key that had been given me. Mrs. Straight was in the study, writing. The fire was bright, the windows blazed with chrysanthemums. Inside like out, suburban serenity. The radio was playing a recording of one of Churchill's "Fight On The

56

Beaches" speeches. I turned the set off and sat down on the arm of the sofa.

"The pendant was either made in France or in Italy."

She put her pen down and looked up, eyes puzzled. "You make it sound important. Is it?"

I lifted my shoulders. "It could be. Tell me something, didn't you say your husband called you every day? If that's right you'd know if the call came from abroad."

Frown lines gathered between her eyes. "I didn't mean it literally. Sometimes a week would go by. I'm not sure I understand your questions."

I swung an armchair in her direction. I wanted her where I could see her face. She sat down obediently. The skin under her eyes was bruised with fatigue. I leaned forward, taking her hands in mine. She made no move to prevent me.

"That pendant was made to order," I said. "My own guess is that he left it with someone, with instructions that it was to be delivered on your wedding anniversary. No manifestations from the dead, just a sick mind's idea of an even sicker joke. Can't you see that, Mrs. Straight?"

She pulled her fingers away, rubbing them furtively. "You'll have to do better than that. What about the music?"

I looked at her meaningfully. "I'm not so sure about the music. Imagination plays strange tricks."

"My God," she said flatly. "And I thought you were going to help me."

The reproach in her eyes haunted me. "What do you *think* I'm trying to do?" I burst out. "OK, it's *not* imagination. Look, when I came into this room, you had the radio playing. Churchill's a long time dead but you were listening to his voice. It could have been your husband's. What's that prove — ectoplasm?"

She studied my face fixedly. "Someone still has to put the record on."

"For Crissakes," I said despairingly. "Isn't that just what I'm saying! We're looking for something more solid than six yards of cheesecloth. Why don't you let me tell Pardoe about all this. I'd feel happier."

She went to the desk slowly and picked up the letter she'd been writing.

"I'd like you to read this." I did.

Dear Edward,

You made your position very clear yesterday, both as a friend and a lawyer. I quite understand that your concern for me goes deeper than your disapproval. Employing Mr. Bain is my responsibility.

Whatever happens now I won't plague you with any more of my fears and fancies. As you've pointed out, they're not evidence.

Sincerely,
Jessica

I gave the letter back to her. She sealed it in an envelope.

"Can't you understand," she pleaded. "I don't *want* to go to him."

That much I understood. I wasn't quite sure about the reason.

"Have it your own way," I said. Maybe it was as well. All we had to offer was a piece of gold on a chain. The thin spiral of smoke from the joss-stick filled the room with the cloying scent of jasmine.

She suddenly looked a lot happier, as if my decision had created a bond of comradeship between us.

"I can't go on calling you 'Mr. Bain,' " she objected. "Do you mind me saying 'Macbeth'?"

"Why not?" I agreed. I'd almost forgotten that I was in the house under false pretenses.

She touched the back of her hair. "Then that's settled. You don't have to answer this. That picture in your room, is it your wife?"

She was nervous in spite of her smile. Nervous and desperately in need of friendship.

"You mean Kirstie," I said. "We're not married yet. I'm still working on it." I could only hope that the Fate Sisters were listening and approved.

She put her manicure set in a small case, nodding understanding. "Then she's a lucky girl as well as a pretty one." Her manner changed abruptly. "About Martha. She's been with me too long to have secrets from her. I had to give some reason for you being here. I told her the truth."

I didn't care one way or another. At least it should stop the maid from slipping arsenic in the soup. I pulled the pendant out of my pocket.

"You'd better put this away somewhere."

She shut it in the desk, leaving the key in the lock. "I feel guilty about your Kirstie. Why not go and see her? You can take the car. I'm going to bed for an hour. I slept so badly."

I opened the door for her. "I'll call her later. Anyway she's at work. I'll be down here if you want me."

She turned her head at the foot of the stairs. "You couldn't have said anything nicer."

A thought struck me as her bedroom door closed. I took the pendant out of the desk and slung it over my wrist. The gold fingers contracted like claws as the chain oscillated. I took it out to the kitchen. Martha was sitting at the table, polishing silver. I showed her the pendant.

"You've seen this before, of course?"

She carried on, burnishing the coffeepot in her lap. "You know I've seen it, don't you. I took the parcel in, two weeks ago yesterday."

I kept my voice casual. "What about the phone calls. Have you heard those, too?"

She suspended her cloth in mid-air, making sure that I took her meaning.

"No, I haven't," she snapped. "Because I was fast asleep in my bed. But I know this much. That villain may be dead but there's others as bad — ready to do his dirty work, torture that poor child out of her mind. It's a police matter, this is. And you ought to be doing something about it."

I dropped the pendant in my pocket. "Suppose I told the police, Martha. They'd be round here asking questions. Have you thought about that?"

"Just what are you getting at, Mister?" she said suspiciously.

I balled my shoulders. "They'd be a lot more inquisitive than I am. They might even think that you know more than you're saying, Martha. Think about it."

Her thin face tightened. "I'll thank you to get out of my kitchen. I'll speak if I'm asked. But it wouldn't be you I'd talk to, make no mistake about it."

I went out through the back door into the fading light. I

took a rake from a shed behind the garage and started raking the leaves off the lawn. I'd been about as tactless as a Jesuit in a synagogue. The list of possible suspects was like my mind, blank. The premise was simple enough. A man hates his wife enough to arrange for a gift to be delivered after his death. A hotel porter could have done it, a messenger service, any one of a thousand people. So why look for a suspect. I didn't have to turn mental somersaults to get the answer. That too was simple. I believed every word of Jessica Straight's story. Somebody *was* calling her and playing that goddammed record. No porter could account for that, no messenger service. I had to find someone with the same warped mind as the late Mr. Straight. Someone with a motive strong enough to make him help wreck a woman's sanity.

For the next hour I raked aimlessly round the garden. The light was going fast. I went back into a warm and silent house. The clock ticked in the empty kitchen. Martha had gone. I pulled the curtains in the study and sat down with the newspapers. I was half-asleep when the phone rang.

I lifted the receiver with a foreboding that was justified. It was Jack the Rat, his voice grotesquely genteel.

"Can I speak to Mr. Bain, please?"

I could hear the cavernous sound of a train dispatcher's announcement in the background. My first impulse was to hang up. He'd only call again. I made the words tell.

"Listen to me, Rowlands. The next time you ring this number I'm going to come after you and beat your brains out."

He made a sort of neighing sound high in his nose. "A nice

thing to hear from a friend, I must say. I told you, mate, things ain't too good. Be reasonable. Friends is for helping one another. If you don't want me visiting you out there, just say so. I'll meet you anywhere you like."

He sounded very sure of himself. The threat was implicit. He had to be stopped, quickly and permanently.

"I'll tell you what you do," I said grimly. "You've got the address — Kowloon, Kingston Hill. Come on over. I'll have the law here waiting for you."

There was a brief pause then his tone was ugly with menace. "We'll see about that, mate. Bye-bye for now."

The door opened from the hall as I put the phone down. Mrs. Straight came in shivering.

"My *God*, it's cold. Why is it that nobody else in this house ever seems to feel it except me? Who was that on the phone?"

"It was for me," I said quickly. "My landlord." I kicked the coals to a blaze and threw a log on the fire.

She showed no more interest, glancing at her watch. "I slept. Do you realize what time it is, Macbeth? Almost seven o'clock! I'll have to start thinking about food again. It never ends, does it?"

It was all strangely domesticated. The two of us alone in the house, her use of my name. I opened the cupboard. I was pretty sure I'd scared off Rowlands but I still needed a scotch.

"Drink?" I asked.

The pendant was back in the desk. She was looking down at it, thoughtfully. She didn't seem to have heard me. She swung round to face me.

"Do you know what I'd like to do with that horrible thing?"

"You'd like to sling it in the fire," I said easily. "Don't. We still need it. Do you want a drink?"

She shut the desk again. "That sounds wonderful. A gin and tonic, please."

A light came on in the cupboard. There was a thermos bucket full of ice and a plate of lemons. I filled a couple of glasses and added ice cubes. I gave her one, lifting my own in salute.

"*Skoal!*"

She put her glass down, half-empty. "It's always a good sign. I mean when I drink. It means I'm contented. Food." She went out to the kitchen.

The evening progressed in exactly the same way as the previous one. We ate a beef casserole in front of the fire with another bottle of the Beaujolais. After dinner we played chess. I can't remember much about the games except that this time she gave me a lot more to do. Once again I was conscious of a strange intimacy, as if after years we were beyond need of conversation. Neither of us noticed the time passing.

Suddenly the phone rang upstairs. Her hand flew to her mouth. She jumped up, overturning the board, pointing at the clock behind me. It was two minutes past eleven.

We ran for the door together. I beat her up the stairs. The phone was still ringing as we reached her bedroom. I grabbed at the receiver. I heard someone cough very softly — a click — the sound of an organ. The opening chord almost deafened me. The volume gradually diminished till the melody line was remote. Then silence.

Jessica was standing against the wall, as if she were nailed to it. I picked the phone up again and dialed the operator.

"This is a police inquiry. I'm speaking from Kingston 1867. Someone just telephoned this number. I want the call traced."

The woman's voice was briskly cooperative. "Hold the line, please." She was back in a few seconds. "Are you there, Kingston? The number is Olmer 296. The subscriber's name is Messenger. Thank you."

Jessica's face was colorless. She rounded the end of the bed and stood in front of the mirror. Her shoulders were shaking.

"Do you know anyone called Messenger?" I asked quickly.

She moved her head from side to side, dumbly.

"It doesn't matter." I got up from the bed and dragged the curtains shut. "Our friend's just made his first real mistake. I'm going down there in the morning, as soon as Martha gets here."

She turned round, shielding her throat with her hands. "I can't help it," she whispered. "I'm terrified."

"Leave your door open and don't worry," I answered. "I'll take care of everything downstairs. Read a book or something. Have you got anything to make you sleep?"

She nodded assent. I went down and checked all the doors and windows. Straight and Pardoe would have to be told, no matter what I'd promised her. But not before I'd been to Olmer. No matter what they decided then, my own position would be stronger. I poured myself another drink and called the Automobile Association from the study. The night service gave me a route. Olmer was in Surrey, three-quarters of an hour out of town. Kirstie's number didn't answer. I went upstairs again. Jessica's light was already out.

"See you in the morning," I called. Silence. I said it once more.

This time she answered. "If there *is* a morning."

It was a hell of a note to go to bed on.

Thursday

IT WAS LIGHT when I awoke. I walked along softly and peeped through her open doorway. She was lying on her side, one arm free of the bedclothes, sleeping soundly. I bathed and dressed and was in the kitchen finishing breakfast when Martha arrived. She came in like a terrier scenting a rat. I wiped my mouth.

"Mrs. Straight's still in bed. I'd let her sleep on if I were you."

She unbuttoned her coat, her mouth thin with disapproval. "Look at the mess you've made on my stove!"

I got up, watching her expression carefully. "Mr. Messenger phoned last night, Martha."

She traded look for look, sniffing. "Never heard of him."

"You will," I promised. "I'm going out. Tell Mrs. Straight I'll be back as soon as I can."

I hit the Guildford bypass, making good time. Most of the traffic was headed in the opposite direction. By ten o'clock I was in Olmer. The village sprawled round a broad expanse of rough turf. Some kids were kicking a football around. Beyond the green, lanes led off into deeply wooded hills. I already knew the address I wanted. The only Messenger listed in the area lived at a place called the Old Forge.

I pulled up outside a gas station. A boy on the pumps pointed out the house. It was on the far side of the green, a two-story building in red brick, completely undistinguished. I drove round and parked outside. An arty sign in the front garden read ANTIQUES.

The upstairs windows were open. Smoke curled from the chimney. I left my hat and coat in the car, pushed the gate open, and walked up the flagged path. The white painted door was ajar. I could see no bell. I called a couple of times. Nobody answered. I stepped forward cautiously, into a large hall overcrowded with furniture. A dachshund waddled down the stairs and turned over on its back, tail brushing the carpet. I gave it a cursory scratch. It wriggled through another doorway. I followed into what was obviously used as a showroom. I'm no expert in antiques but the display seemed impressive. There was a Jacobean table and matching set of chairs, Georgian silver and Welsh pewter, a couple of Aubusson carpets on the polished floorboards. The mantel was decked with Staffordshire pottery. A ship's bell hung on a leather strap from one of the beams. The inscription in the bronze was still legible. H.M.S. VALIANT 1707.

The dachshund barked suddenly. I swung my head round, catching it on the side of the bell. The boom echoed throughout the house. I was rubbing my scalp when a woman came in from the hall. She was tall and heavily built with white hair dragged into a bun. She wore a brown alpaca dress and two ropes of beads, low buckled shoes. She must have been well over sixty but her eyes were those of a girl, dark blue and very clear. She clapped her hands softly, chasing the dog from the room and smiling apology.

"I'm so sorry. I didn't hear you come in."

67

"Could I speak to Mr. Messenger," I asked.

Her smile was as untroubled as her eyes. "I'm afraid that's impossible. There *isn't* a Mr. Messenger. I'm Miss Messenger. Will I do?"

The revelation came as a complete surprise. I hadn't expected to be dealing with a woman.

"I'm from the G.P.O. Investigation Branch, Miss Messenger. Does anyone use your telephone except you?"

Her smile faded to a look of puzzlement. "No," she said slowly. "I have a woman in to clean every afternoon. She makes the odd call. The butcher, that sort of thing."

I nodded. "But not at eleven o'clock at night?"

She took a deep breath. "May I ask why you're putting these questions to me?"

It was time for a show of authority. "I'm investigating a series of calls that have been traced to your number. They're of a malicious nature, they've caused worry and concern to the receiver. Let me ask you this, Miss Messenger, does the name Mrs. Straight mean anything to you?"

She sank into a chair, her back erect, hands clasped in her lap.

"I see. Obviously you don't understand. None of these calls was made maliciously — quite the contrary. I'm sad to hear that Mrs. Straight was upset. That'll all change, of course. It's simply a matter of getting her in the right frame of mind."

I took another look at her. She was teasing a bit of stuff from the seam of her dress. I wasn't sure that I'd heard correctly.

"Did you say 'right frame of mind'?" I asked incredulously.

She lifted her head, her manner gentle and restrained. "Exactly. You're probably not aware that her husband passed over some months ago?"

I pulled a pack of cigarettes from my pocket and showed it to her. She moved her head permissively. I lit one and dragged the salt burn deep into my lungs.

"Suppose we get back to these calls you've been making," I suggested.

Her eyes were kind but speculative. "What a pity you're not a believer," she said suddenly. "You're a born healer. I can see the aura."

I made my tone deliberately stern. "I'm a post office investigator, Miss Messenger. What I suggest is that you treat me like one."

She left the room. I heard her moving about overhead. She came down again, carrying a record. She gave it to me. The disc was a duplicate of the one in Mrs. Straight's study. Miss Messenger sat down, crossing her feet neatly at the ankles. She looked about as esoteric as a district nurse.

"I'm a Spiritualist," she said quietly. "Mark Straight was a member of our small circle. He came here one day last spring. It must have been some time in March. I won't try to describe his distress. I prefer not to remember it. I realized afterward that he must have known then what he intended to do. He brought this record with him. You see, music had always been a strong bond between himself and his wife. He asked me to help should anything ever happen to him. He wanted this record played over the telephone to Mrs. Straight, round about the time of their wedding anniversary. I've respected his wishes from a sense of Christian duty."

69

She might have been describing the proceedings at a meeting of the local parish council. I blew a stream of smoke at the floor. It was difficult to square the facts with her quiet innocence.

"Can't you imagine what you've done to an impressionable woman, Miss Messenger, someone only too conscious that her husband committed suicide? Do you seriously contend that you thought you were helping her?"

She unclasped her hands, her eyes steadfast. "I was helping both of them. With time and with prayer, Mrs. Straight will understand that love conquers death, that her husband is truly alive today and that he needs her help."

I put my cigarette out. This gentle fanatic believed every word she said.

"Did Mark Straight give you a package to mail as well?"

Her eyes were as naïve as a child's. "No."

I came to my feet. I couldn't help feeling sorry for her. "All right, Miss Messenger. I'm afraid I'll have to take this record with me. I'll have to make my report, of course. But I wouldn't think you'll hear anything more about this."

She didn't appear concerned, one way or another. "Will you be seeing Mrs. Straight again?"

I stopped at the door. "I expect so, yes. What makes you ask?"

She touched her beads hesitantly. "Please tell her how much I grieve for her. You see, those driven to suicide are the loneliest of all at first. It's very hard for them to come back. They need constant prayer and help. Will you tell her that?"

"I'll pass your message on," I answered. "Thank you for being so frank. Good-bye."

I left her clutching the dog to her breast. I made a left turn and called Pardoe's office from the booth outside the gas station. I stared back at the house, receiver tucked under my chin, waiting for the connection. A cultured middle-aged woman, conducting a business, carrying on a life that was to all intents and purposes a normal one. Yet for the better part of two weeks, she'd been broadcasting organ music to a stranger and saw no harm in it.

The girl took my name. Pardoe came on the line immediately. He sounded in a hurry.

"Can you make it brief?" he asked. "I'm in the middle of an important conference."

I heard him excuse himself to someone in the room. "What can I do for you, Bain?" he inquired.

"You'd better see me as soon as possible," I answered. "I don't want to discuss it over the phone. I'm down in the country. It'll take me an hour to get back to town."

"I see," he said cautiously. "There's nothing wrong, is there?"

"I'd say there's a great deal wrong," I replied. "But I'll let you decide about that."

"I'll wait here for you," he said. "Be as quick as you can." He hung up.

I dialed the Kingston number. As soon as I heard her voice I knew something had happened.

"What is it?" I asked quickly.

Her courage seemed to drain with each word. "A man just brought some flowers."

The news sounded so banal that I didn't bother to hide my irritation.

"Well for God's sake, what of it?" I demanded.

The seconds stretched before she answered. "There was a card with them — in his handwriting."

"Never mind all that," I said reassuringly. "I've got the answers to everything. Is there an address on the wrapping?"

She read it out. I wrote the details on a piece of paper. "Now you get a hold on yourself," I said. "Pour yourself the largest drink you can and get ready for some good news. I'll be back in a couple of hours."

The phone dangled uselessly in my hand. She wasn't listening anymore.

It was ten to one at King's Bench Walk. Straight had either been there when I phoned or Pardoe had sent for him. The Mercedes was parked behind the Bentley. I left the Mini round the corner and hurried into the office. The girl passed me through into the big room filled with cigar smoke. There was a sherry bottle and a couple of glasses on a table by the safe. Straight was standing with his back to the window, wearing the same gray tweeds and a black knitted tie. Pardoe was behind the desk, impressive in a double-breasted jacket and wing-collar. He'd have been halfway to an acquittal on appearance alone. He waved a hand at the chair in front of him.

I sat down, bracing my back against the hard wood. "You're not going to like this but Mrs. Straight's no more crazy than I am. Here, put this in your safe. It's part of your late client's estate." I threw the record on the desk in front of him.

Both men stared at the colored jacket as if only close inspection could give my words meaning. Pardoe spoke into the intercom box.

"See that I'm not disturbed, Miss Banks. And that means for anything."

He flipped up the switch and considered me narrowly. "I think you'd better explain yourself."

"I'll do just that," I said steadily. "Mark Straight ought to have been locked up years ago. The guy was insane — a head case."

I'd rehearsed the story on the way up from Olmer. I nailed fact to fact. The delivery of the pendant, the telephone calls, the bizarre Miss Messenger. Last of all the flowers. Pardoe's florid face reddened even more. He kept sneaking a sideways look at Straight, whether for guidance or rebuttal I didn't know. Straight paid no attention to him. He leaned against a bookcase, watching me with a fixed, impassive stare.

I stopped and lit a cigarette. I'd been talking for the best part of fifteen minutes. Neither of them had spoken. I dropped the matches in my pocket and blew a spiral of smoke.

"OK, there it is. I've come about as far as I can on my own. Someone else has got to help wind up this production."

Straight poured himself a glass of sherry. He took it to the window and stood there sniffing the bouquet. Pardoe cleared his throat noisily.

"You seem to have shown a remarkable degree of resourcefulness already. If what you say is true," he added.

I felt the old slow burn rising, the failing that was doomed to stay with me.

"I wouldn't like to think you're calling me a liar."

Straight whirled round, throwing a hand out. "Nobody's

73

calling you a liar, Mr. Bain. The truth is that we're both too stunned to talk reasonably. My brother's behavior was a source of worry long before his death. I'm afraid what you've told us only confirms my suspicions."

"That's hardly what you gave me to understand," I volunteered.

"I'm aware of it," he said. "You're forgetting that he was my brother."

I wasn't likely to forget. His concern was obviously for the dead rather than the living.

"It might have been easier," I said, "if you'd both been a little franker with me. Maybe you've forgotten what you said. The idea was that Mrs. Straight was the one who was unbalanced, not your brother."

"It's not an easy thing to say to a stranger." Neither his voice nor his manner carried me. He'd been less delicate about his sister-in-law's interests.

"Maybe not," I agreed. "Even less easy to admit when the stranger finds out for himself."

Straight put his empty glass down. "I think you're right. Don't you think he's right, Edward?"

I had the oddest feeling that they were talking about something else entirely. Pardoe shifted in his chair.

"I expect that Mr. Bain feels that he's done everything that could be expected of him. I agree, I can't see there's any more that he can do. I suggest we pay him the money we promised him and deal with this situation ourselves."

Straight smiled bleakly. "Suppose we ask Mr. Bain what *he* thinks. How about it, Mr. Bain. Would you take your check and go and feel perfectly happy?"

I hesitated. "I hired out for a job. You promised me a

74

certain sum of money. If the job's over I'd like to be paid. It's as simple as that. What am I supposed to feel happy about?"

Pardoe pulled a checkbook from a drawer. "The job *is* over and you *are* going to be paid. I'll make this out to bearer, will that be all right?"

Straight reached over, taking the pen from Pardoe's fingers. His face was like a wax model.

"You take too much for granted," he said icily. "I make the decisions, not you. I asked you a question, Mr. Bain. I'm not welching. You'll get your money. But I must know something first. Which do you think it is that really worries me — my brother's memory or his wife's peace of mind?"

"A little of both," I said frankly. "My guess is that I've become an embarrassment to you. That's because you don't know me. Let me tell you this. The moment you say I'm through, I'm going to forget anything I saw or heard. But it doesn't mean I haven't the right to an opinion. And I'm going to give it to you. You had a desperately frightened woman on your hands and you didn't show her one ounce of understanding or compassion."

Straight lifted a hand in token admission. "We both made a mistake."

"You might as well know this much," I added. "Nothing that's been said in this office is going to stop me from telling her the truth. Your brother was a diabolical bastard. It's a pity you can't tell her yourself. It might have been fairer. But I realize that's out of the question. I'm forty pounds ahead of the game. Do what you like with the rest of it."

Pardoe glanced up at Straight, his expression wry. "You got your answer. Are you satisfied?"

"I'm satisfied," Straight said evenly. "Now I'll tell *you*

75

something, Mr. Bain. You *are* an embarrassment. But I respect you. And I do care about the damage done to an innocent woman. That's why I'm asking you to help her as long as she needs it. Let *her* be the judge of how long that is. You can't spare my brother's memory as far as she is concerned. But for others you can. I'll be grateful if you will."

There was no attempt to threaten or cajole. Just a man made vulnerable by circumstance. His dignity decided me.

"Fair enough," I said. "I'll do what I can. There'll be no scandal if I can help it. But you're going to have to keep well out of the way — both of you."

"We will," Straight promised quickly. "My sister-in-law trusts you. So do I. I'm sure you'll have the right ideas. I don't have to tell you that fears of this kind die hard. It won't be easy for her."

"It wouldn't be easy for anyone," I replied. "She's got to start living again. And when the time comes, she'll need your help more than mine. I'm talking about money. The best thing she could do is get on a slow boat and forget that house ever existed."

Straight moved his head in agreement. "I'd been thinking along those lines myself. Everything will be done for her, you have my word on that. Naturally, she won't know I have anything to do with it. Pardoe and I will work something out between us."

I picked my hat and coat up. "Then I'd better get back to her. I'd sooner she doesn't know that I've been here. It can only weaken my position."

"We're entirely in your hands," Straight said. "You have my telephone number. Don't hesitate to use it if you feel that it's necessary. What are you doing about the florist?"

I shrugged into my coat. "I haven't made my mind up yet. Certainly I'm going to talk to him."

He nodded good-bye. Pardoe came to the outside door with me. The two offices were empty, the staff at lunch. He hung onto the doorhandle, looking at me meaningfully.

"Don't leave her alone," he said in a low voice and was gone.

I drove west to Brompton Road. It was a quarter of an hour before I found a place to park. The florist shop was halfway down Beauchamp Place, between a hat shop and a poodle parlor. The front window was a blaze of long-stemmed roses. I stepped into a warm steamy atmosphere, heavy with the scent of freesias.

A man rose from a gilt and white desk. He was very gray and as willowy as one of his flowers. I wasted no time on preliminaries.

"You delivered some lilies this morning to a Mrs. Jessica Straight. I want to know who sent them."

He gave a little skip sideways, his voice shocked. "I'm afraid we don't divulge information about our customers' transactions, sir."

Someone was moving round in the back of the premises. I pitched my voice a little higher.

"Maybe not. But you'll make an exception. I'm the lady's husband."

His eyes rounded. "I see," he said warily. "Well, in that case, perhaps. What was the address, sir?"

I gave it to him very distinctly. He flicked through the pages, wagging his head. Suddenly he stopped. "Kowloon. Putney Hill. Here it is. A dozen arum lilies to be delivered this morning."

"Who ordered them?" I demanded.

He seemed to hesitate. I whipped the book out of his hand. There was no sender's name, nothing but the price, date, and description of flowers. I threw the book back on the table.

He drew himself up indignantly. "Well, *really!*"

I caught him by the lapel. "Now you listen to me very carefully. I'm sure you don't want to be involved in a lot of unpleasantness?"

He removed my hand with a pained expression. "This is a highly respectable business, sir."

"Then you'll want to keep it that way," I said. "Think again. There was a card enclosed with those flowers. Who sent it?"

He ran his fingers lightly over his head, glancing into the mirror for reassurance.

"Whoever it was must have paid cash. Otherwise there'd be a record of it." He called over his shoulder.

A diminutive girl in a blue nylon smock appeared, drying wet hands.

"Yes, Mr. Lance?"

He showed her the entry in the order book. "Can you remember this customer, dear? It's your writing. It must have been sometime in August when I was on holiday."

She nodded briskly. "I remember, yes. It was a taxi driver. Why, is there something wrong?"

"Nothing wrong, dear," the florist said hastily. "We just wondered if he'd left a name."

"Just the money and the card," she replied.

He smiled brilliantly. "Thank you, Janet. Don't forget

Mrs. Ogilvie's order, will you, dear. Long stems and lots of buds. You know." He pantomimed despair behind her retreating back. "You've got to be so careful with them," he confided. "The simplest thing and they take offense. I'm afraid I can't do anything more for you, sir."

It was little enough. Mark Straight would have been dead five months when the flowers were delivered. But he could still have arranged it. By the time I'd battled my way through Putney and across Wimbledon Common, it was almost half past three. I was halfway up the hill when I saw Martha coming down. She was dressed in her street clothes, skinny legs thrust into high boots, her ginger hair in a turban hat.

I stopped the car and wound the window down. "Where are you off to?"

She looked at me resentfully. "Home, that's where."

She was an hour ahead of schedule. There had to be a reason. I glanced at my watch meaningfully.

"A bit early, isn't it?"

Her peaked face was stony. "I do what I'm told, mister. She wanted to be alone."

"Where is she?" I asked quickly.

Her manner was reticent. "In her bedroom. She was lying down. A man telephoned after lunch. He said it was important so I called her. She's been upstairs ever since."

I had a strong sense of foreboding. "Was his name Rowlands?"

I switched on the motor, not waiting for the answer. Her eyes had already given it to me. I left the car in the driveway and ran up the stairs. Her bedroom door was locked. I rapped on it, softly at first and then louder. There was no reply. I stepped back and charged the door with my shoulder. The entire house seemed to shake under the impact but the lock held. I raced down the stairs, skidded across the hall, and made for the shed behind the garage. A ladder was suspended from the rafters. I hauled it down and dragged it to the wall beneath her windows. The ladder sagged under my weight, sinking deep into the wet earth. I clambered up till my feet were on the top rung. I teetered there, reaching up for the sill. My legs dangled in space. I hauled myself up, pain pumping in tortured muscles. I just managed to grab the sash, crouched on the sill, and went through, landing on hands and knees.

I looked over at the bed. She was lying fully dressed, her left arm trailing loosely. A wisp of ashen hair hid her mouth and nose. It lifted and fell with her stertorous breathing. There was an empty glass on the table beside her, a small bottle next to it. This too was empty. I read the printed label. *To be taken as ordered. It is dangerous to exceed the prescribed dosage.*

I put my arms under her body, lifting her higher in the pillows. She sagged in my grip, eyes closed, mouth half-open. Sleep had passed into coma. Her hands and feet were cold, her body losing its warmth. Her handbag was on the dresser. I tore it open frantically. A prescription was tucked into the wallet. I dialed the number on the heading. A woman answered.

"Good afternoon. Doctor Verney's surgery."

"I've got to talk with the doctor," I said urgently. "This is an emergency."

The seconds stretched, the only sound in the room the labored breathing behind me. Then a man's voice.

"Doctor Verney. Who is it speaking?"

"Don't waste time," I answered desperately. *"Get here!* Mrs. Straight, Kowloon, Kingston Hill. She's just swallowed a bottle of sleeping pills."

He gave the instructions calmly. "Wrap her up well. Put some hot-water bottles on her feet, anything you can find. I'll be there in five minutes."

I bundled her in the bedding and unlocked the door. A couple of hot-water bottles were hanging in a closet in the kitchen. I filled them and ran back upstairs. I packed the bottles in the eiderdown and put her feet on them. Her hands and wrists were icy. A car pulled up outside. I raced down again and opened the front door. A youngish man with graying hair brushed past me, opening his bag as he climbed the stairs. He was already at work by the time I reached the bedroom. A deft hand felt her pulse, lifted an eyelid. He dragged the blankets down and sounded her heart with a stethoscope. He whipped a hypodermic syringe from his bag, inserting the needle in the neck of a vial. Steady fingers pulled the plunger back. The liquid sank slowly into the syringe. He looked up at me, his eyes troubled.

"How long since she took these pills?"

I shook my head. "I don't know. An hour, maybe. I just don't know."

He pulled up her left sleeve, dabbed the inside of her arm, and inserted the needle in the vein. His thumb depressed the plunger, feeding the injection into the bloodstream. He fitted the syringe to another vial and found a fresh spot in the vein.

81

He dropped her arm and sounded her heart again.

"Make coffee," he ordered suddenly. "As strong as you can and hot. Never mind the sugar."

I hurried down to the kitchen. Anything was better than just standing there, watching her helplessness. I brewed the coffee as he'd said and carried it up to the bedroom. He rose to his feet slowly, putting his stethoscope away in an inside pocket.

"She'll do," he said shortly. "Give me a hand to get her up."

We slipped pillows behind her back, pulling her into a sitting position. Her eyes opened hazily. She looked at me without recognition, wiping the damp hair from her forehead. Verney held the steaming cup under her nose.

"Slowly now," he warned. "It's hot."

She took the cup in her hands, the tears running down her cheeks.

"It's all right," he soothed. "There's nothing to worry about. It's all right." He moved his head toward the door significantly.

I went to my own room and sat down, staring through the window with a deep sense of depression. I could hear her talking to the doctor. I thought vaguely of packing my bag and sneaking out. It wouldn't have changed anything. I knew that I was partly responsible for her attempt at suicide. Learning the truth about me had been the back breaker. I could go but I'd carry the memory with me. One way or another I had to face her.

I looked round, hearing the steps along the corridor. Verney came into the room and put his bag on the floor.

"She'll be all right," he said casually. "I understand that you're staying in the house, Mister . . . ?"

"Bain." I averted my eyes. "I'm not sure how long for."

"She mustn't be left alone," he put in quickly. "How long have you known her, Mr. Bain?"

"Not long," I answered.

He picked a shred of lint from his jacket, still casual. "She's only been in my care since June. Have you any idea how long she's been a widow?"

"Since March," I told him. "Her husband committed suicide."

He whistled softly. "That accounts for a lot. I wish I'd known before. She's an extremely difficult patient. Highstrung, almost pathologically reserved. Please don't think me impertinent but how close to her *are* you?"

I looked at him steadily. "I'm a friend, Doctor. No more no less."

He accepted the rebuke, frowning. "There's a reason for asking. In my opinion she needs very careful handling. Above all she needs someone to confide in — someone she trusts implicitly. I'd suggest a good psychiatrist. I believe there's a lawyer somewhere in the background, isn't there? It might be as well if you had a word with him. He can always get in touch with me."

"I'll do that." I said hurriedly. "I've got to ask you this, Doctor, for my own peace of mind. Is she likely to try it again?"

He made a quick gesture of dissent. "I wouldn't think there's much chance of it. There's another aspect to consider. Accidents happen frequently under sedation. A patient takes a normal dose, wakes from a doze and takes another without even being conscious of it."

His face was earnest and he sounded sincere. But I sensed he was letting us off the hook. Himself, too, for all I knew.

"You'd better tell me what to do, Doctor," I suggested.

He picked his bag up, swinging it thoughtfully. "The chief thing's to keep barbiturates out of her reach. I've left her some pills but they're harmless. I wouldn't tell her that, though. I'll drop by in the morning. You have my number if you need me." He jerked his head back along the corridor. "She wants to see you."

I went to the front door with him, waiting till his car was out of sight. It seemed a long long walk back up to her room.

The windows were shut and the heater was on. She'd washed her face and brushed her hair. She was sitting up in bed. I sat down near her feet.

"This isn't going to be easy for either of us, Jessica. I don't have any excuses. The main thing is that you were right and everyone else was wrong. There's no mystery anymore. Quite simply it was your husband. He fixed everything before his death. The pendant, the phone calls, the flowers. I'll give you all the details. You can't be alone. I'll stay till the morning, of course."

She lifted a hand to her hair. Her sleeve slipped back. Gauze covered the punctures in the hollow of her elbow.

"Doctor Verney says that you saved my life. I'm grateful for it, Macbeth. I want to live and I want you to stay."

I took a deep breath. "Didn't Rowlands tell you — I'm a convicted thief?"

Her face was washed of everything but truth. "I still want you to stay."

"It wouldn't work," I objected. Deep down I wanted her to deny it, for my sake not hers.

"Why not?" she asked simply. "I know what I'm doing. Stay at least for a while. Tell me something. Does Kirstie know about your past?"

That much no one could take from me. "She knows," I said.

She brooded for a moment. "That's what I thought. Do something for me, Macbeth. Take the car and go and see her tonight. Tell her what has happened, that I'm asking you to stay for a while. I think she'll understand."

"It wouldn't work," I repeated. "The man who called you won't stop there. He'll track down everyone connected with you. Finally he'll get to Pardoe."

She hitched the robe round her shoulders. "I already thought of that. I got in first. I just talked to Edward. I told him that if you'd been going to rob me, you'd have done it before now. Speak to him yourself if you like but don't let him browbeat you. The main thing is I *want* you here."

The words lifted my feeling of depression. There was still something unfinished between us. I wasn't sure what. I knew I had a deep compassion for her. Suddenly I remembered a scene from long ago — a French jail, the man who'd lived in the cell next to mine. An old man, foul and friendless. He had no visitors, received no mail. One night he rapped on the wall. I was on my bed, reading. The rapping grew desperate. I still ignored it. Then it stopped. It was his last attempt to communicate. The guards cut him down three hours later, hanging from the bars by his belt. I'd never completely forgotten that a kick on the wall could have saved his life. Hers must have been the same despair, the same feeling of utter loneliness.

"You're an obstinate woman," I said. "I'll stay."

Her violet eyes were huge and shadowed. "First go and see Kirstie. It's important to me. I'll sleep. Doctor Verney left me some pills."

I hesitated. Verney's instructions had been explicit. "I don't think I ought to leave you."

"Nonsense," she said determinedly. "What are you going to do, sit there and watch me sleep? For God's sake, Macbeth! I'm starting to *live* again, remember."

It was hard to argue with her in this mood. "Have it your way," I said. "I won't be gone long."

She managed to smile. "That's better. Now give me my bag."

She took out her address book and scribbled on a piece of paper.

"Here's Martha's address. You can drop in on your way. Tell her not to come tomorrow. I'd sooner be alone with you. Remember what we said about laying ghosts? I want to hear just how evil my husband really was. I might even laugh about it but I certainly don't want an audience."

I put her handbag back on the dresser. "I'm not exactly wild about the prospect of phoning Pardoe."

"Then don't," she said shortly. "He's got nothing to do with it, anyway."

I couldn't help wondering just how much she'd told him. She wrapped her knees in the eiderdown, looking at me curiously.

86

"He knows what I did, if that's what's worrying you. And he knows that you saved my life."

"I'll call him from downstairs," I said. I managed to catch Pardoe's secretary. He'd already left for home. I searched my pockets for John Straight's number. She was as much their problem as mine. I lifted the receiver and redialed. He came on, sounding oddly at ease.

"I'd rather been expecting you to call. I've just had Pardoe on the phone, worrying about your police record instead of my sister-in-law. How is she?"

"She's all right now." I took a grip on the receiver. "I've already made my apologies. There's nothing else to add except that she's asked me to stay on."

"Why not?" he observed. "I can't think of anything better, at least for the moment."

"That's big of you." I couldn't resist the sarcasm. He was too easy, too urbane.

His manner changed abruptly. "You don't appear to understand. I'm concerned about a woman in distress. The details of your past don't really interest me. Are you staying or not?"

"I'm staying," I said curtly.

"Good," he said reasonably. "I'm not going to pretend that I like the situation. But then I don't suppose you do. There's nothing much we can do about it. What does the doctor say?"

I told him and added, "He's coming again in the morning. He said something about a psychiatrist. All she wants to do is sleep."

"Probably the best thing for her," he answered. "In any case you'll be there if she needs you."

The way he said it got under my skin. It was an order rather than a request, an assumption that the ex-con would be knuckling his forehead with gratitude.

"I'm going out for a while," I said distinctly. "On a personal matter. It's her idea, not mine. I won't be gone long, no later than nine."

He sounded a little dubious. "I suppose it's a sort of challenge. Being left alone, I mean. You're quite sure she'll be all right?"

"I wouldn't be leaving her otherwise."

"Of course not," he hurried. "Call me again in the morning. As soon as the doctor's been there. And listen, Bain, I wouldn't bother trying to explain to Pardoe. It'll be better if you let me handle it."

"Whatever you say," I replied and put the receiver down. At least he was realistic. I took the papers out to the kitchen. The cat jumped down from its cushion, eyeing me apprehensively. I laid a tray with milk, fruit, and cheese. The cat followed me upstairs. It jumped onto the foot of her bed and settled down, kneading the eiderdown. Jessica was leaning back in a nest of pillows. I placed the tray across her lap. She'd used scent since I'd left the room.

"Shall I tell you what he said?" she queried.

I unfolded the newspapers. "Pardoe? I didn't speak to him. He'd already left the office." If she asked me who I *had* spoken to, I was going to have to tell her. I was through lying. She had her own part to play now in facing reality. And Mark's brother or not, John Straight was reality.

She let it go, polishing an apple with a corner of the sheet. "I've been thinking, Macbeth. You'd better let me edit your story for Kirstie. I'm a woman — I know. The last thing I want is to be the cause of trouble between you."

I let the bait float by before taking it. "What makes you think there'll be trouble?"

"Jealousy," she said, looking at me meaningfully.

Her expression disturbed me. "Now wait a minute," I objected. "Kirstie's got no reason to be jealous and she knows it."

She sank her teeth into the apple, grimaced and put it back on the plate.

"Would you take the tray, please. I'm not hungry."

I put the tray on the floor and sealed a chink in the curtains. She was still looking at me enigmatically when I turned round.

"Don't be alarmed. I'm not asking for anything that belongs to her, Macbeth. I'm asking for comradeship, not sex. Don't you have any to spare?"

Instinct told me this was dangerous ground. She'd centered her need of human contact on me. I switched all the lights off except the one over her head.

"I'm surprised you ask. I'd have thought that was one thing that had been established. I'd better go now. I don't want to be late. Try to get some sleep."

She stretched and yawned. "I think I will. You go. I don't want you to worry about me. Enjoy yourself." Her voice was suddenly small and humble. "That's not really true. I *want* you to worry about me. Is that so terrible, Macbeth?"

I could have taken her in my arms, atonement for a thousand rejections of her pity. I was afraid of what might happen. Innocence of intent would help neither of us.

"Sleep well," I answered. "I'll look in when I get back. I won't be long."

I went down, screened the fires and left the hall lights burning. I looked up at her windows from the front steps. They were already in darkness.

I backed the car out between trees rising in the wind. I located Martha's flat in a council-block on the south side of Putney Bridge. I found her on the second floor. She let me into a living room a quarter of the size of her kitchen. It was just as surgically clean and neat. An armchair was drawn up in front of the television set. She switched off the sound, looking at me suspiciously. I gave her Jessica's instructions, saying nothing about the attempted suicide. Jessica would have to deal with that in her own way. The maid's manner made it plain that she took the news as an insult engineered by me. She started making objections that there was laundry to prepare, food to be ordered for the weekend.

I glanced at my watch impatiently. There'd be little enough time with Kirstie as it was.

"Why not just do as you're told," I said sharply. "You're not wanted tomorrow and that's all there is to it."

The door was slammed hard behind me. I headed the Mini east towards Chelsea. Kirstie's Volkswagen was in the unloading bay at the rear of the post office. Flush against the radiator was a sign reading NO PARKING EXCEPT FOR G.P.O. VEHICLES.

God knows how she got away with it. She'd had her car hauled away seven times already. She figured that, spread over time, the fines she paid to collect it from the police pound were economical. I ran the Mini alongside and walked up to the apartment. The record player was going. I buzzed the bell twice. The music stopped. Her head came round the door. She peered up at me from under a dark brown fringe. She made her eyes round with astonishment.

"Well if it isn't Mr. Bain! Are you out on parole or something?"

I lifted her solid little body off the ground and carried her into the sitting room. I dropped her in the middle of the records scattered over the carpet. She'd been eating in front of the fire. There was an empty milk glass on the floor, the remains of a toasted cheese sandwich.

I looked her up and down carefully. "What are you supposed to be dressed for — *Swan Lake*?"

She smoothed the short kilted skirt complacently. "Nice, isn't it? I bought it yesterday. I've already had a lot of success with it at the office."

I unfastened the drinks cupboard and poured myself a scotch. "I'm sure you have. What happens if you drop something?"

She shook her hair back, smiling secretly. "When I drop things, darling, someone else picks them up."

I raised my glass. "Chivalry. Long may it last. Listen, there's a lot to say and not much time to do it in."

She swept the records into a pile and plumped herself into an armchair. She composed her arms gracefully, one hand supporting her chin. Lady Windermere without the fan.

"I'm grateful for whatever time you can spare," she said.

I dragged the other chair over. Our knees were touching. "You — are — being — very — stupid," I said distinctly. "Do you want to hear or not?"

She pulled her legs away and tucked them under her. She blew a cloud of smoke at me.

"I'm listening, you rat," she said grimly.

"I love you when you're like this," I said, shaking my head. "Those hazel eyes full of love and adoration. You're burying the hatchet, again, in my back."

"Just tell the story," she said calmly. "I know it's going to be good."

She had a talent for making me feel like a liar even before I opened my mouth. It would have been the same if I'd been reading from the Gospels. It was a trick that she had and there was nothing I could do about it. I launched myself back in time doggedly. She listened without offering a word. I kept hoping for a flicker of interest or sympathy. She just sat silent with narrowed eyes. I plowed on to the end.

"I had to tell you. And don't waste your time with the lecture about basic dishonesty. I've heard it all before, remember? If I hadn't told lies to get the job none of this would have happened, et cetera. The thing is that these people know the worst and they want me to stay."

She unfolded her legs, picked the plate and glass from the floor and took them out to the kitchen. I poured myself another scotch while she was out of the room. She came back and sat down, pointing her finger at me.

"We're going to return the lady's car," she said steadily. "I'm coming with you. You'll collect your things and say good night and *that will be that!*"

I finished the last of my drink before answering. "You're out of your fool mind if you think *I'm* going to walk away from money I've earned, Kirstie."

"That's what it is, the money?" she demanded.

I spread my hands wide. "For Crissakes, Kirstie, the woman needs help."

She stretched her hand out. "Give me a drink."

I half-filled a glass with port. She sniffed it, wrinkling her snub nose.

"It won't be for long," I urged. "A couple of weeks only, till she adjusts."

She put her glass down violently. "I know the sort of help she needs. She's just desperate for a man. And she thinks she's found one. You don't suppose she cares whether you've been to prison! 'Saved her life!' Don't be so naïve. The whole thing was staged to get your attention."

"You heartless little bitch," I said steadily. "I love you but I'm not buying it. I am *not* walking out on her."

She was dangerously quiet, suddenly, twisting our ring round on her finger.

"I see. Then you'd better start learning about love before it's too late, Macbeth."

I put my hand under her chin, forcing her head up. "Are you telling me I haven't learned?" Her lips were unresponsive, her eyes defiant. I knew the mood only too well. The longer I stayed, the worse it would get. I let her go. "Of all people I hoped at least *you* would understand. I'm sorry. I'll call you first thing in the morning. I'm going to tell her there's got to be a limit on my stay. No more than two weeks. OK?"

She wiped her eyes furiously. "Oh, for God's sake, get back! I'm sick of sitting here talking about her. You're behaving like a character in a comic strip."

She'd surrendered but the surrender would cost me dearly. I picked up my coat.

93

"Is that how we say good night?" She looked at me without answering. I shrugged. "I'll call you in the morning."

"Please yourself," she said stonily and made no move to come to the door with me.

I let myself out and hurried down to the car. It was half past eight by the clock in St. Luke's churchyard. The odd thing is that if she hadn't given in — if she'd presented me with the choice between herself and Jessica — I'd have done as she wanted. Gone back with her and claimed my bag. I think that deep down, she accepted the fact that I was trying to prove something to myself. But as far as I was concerned, I was doing the only thing possible for both of us.

I drove carefully, remembering the scotch. It was no time to be picked up and given a breathalyzer test. The long rise of Kingston Hill showed in the headlights. I turned off onto the driveway and put the car away in the garage. Jessica's room was in darkness. I made no noise opening the front door. The cat stalked out of the kitchen, mewing. I deposited it in the garden and went up the stairs. Her bedroom door was open. I tiptoed along the corridor and peeped in. It was too dark to see her face but she was lying on her side breathing regularly.

I ran a bath, soaking for half an hour in the hot scented water. I'd eaten little enough during the day but I wasn't hungry. I couldn't get Kirstie's face out of my mind. The wistful stubborn look as I vanished through her door. I dried myself and scrambled into bed. You couldn't win them all.

Friday

I WOKE to the chatter of blackbirds on the front lawn. I rolled over, making an arm for my watch. Nearly half past seven. I was dressed and shaved by eight. Kirstie's picture was reproachful from the dressing table. It was early to call her and I wanted to speak to Jessica first. There was no sound from her room. She must have been sleeping for the better part of twelve hours. No Martha there meant that I was cook. I might as well find out what she wanted for breakfast.

My first impression was that the room was oppressively hot. The heater was still burning. I switched it off and dragged the curtains back. The bathroom door was open. Drawers gaped in the tallboy. The bed was unnaturally still in the pale light of day. I could see her clearly now. The bedclothes were down round her waist. She was lying on her back with her arms crossed on her stomach. Her mouth had dropped as if in one last gasp for air. A car's motor revved in a nearby driveway. I don't know how long I stood there before bringing myself to take the five steps to the bed. I circled her wrist with my fingers. Her hand was icy cold. There was no pulse. I released my grip. Her arm fell uselessly.

I picked the phone up, trailing a length of cut cord. Someone had severed the line near the wall. I ran down the stairs, my brain registering impressions through a felt curtain. The rattle of the flap in the front door, the newspapers landing on the hall mat. I heard the boy outside whistling his way down the steps. I opened the study door. The curtains were still drawn. The first thing I noticed was the portrait on the floor. The safe door was wide open, the key in the lock.

I sat down and composed Straight's number. It rang without answer. I dialed the operator. He *had* to reply.

"If you'll hold the line," she said nasally, "I will try again for you."

The hand holding the mouthpiece was shaking. A double buzz spaced the silence in the earphone. Then I heard his voice, sleepy and relaxed.

"Six-seven-four-seven."

"This time she's done it properly," I said flatly. "She's dead."

His tone sharpened with incredulity. "*What?*"

"She's dead," I repeated. "You'd better get over here fast."

"Have you called the doctor?" he asked quickly.

"She doesn't need a doctor," I replied. "I'm going to call the police."

He hammered the words at me. "Stay where you are. Don't leave the house till I get there. Call nobody and don't touch the body. I'm sure it's important."

I lifted my head slowly. The advice was superfluous. I didn't even want to look at her again, let alone touch her. I crossed the room to the safe. Empty jewel cases were scattered over the bottom shelf. I could only think of Jack the Rat. I pictured him lying in the bushes, watching me leave the house. I'd locked all the doors but the windows were burglar-proof in name only. It was easy to put an elbow through a pane of glass.

I pulled the curtains back. The panes were intact. I went into the drawing room. I didn't have to look far. A jagged hole showed in the French windows, just over the doorhandle. The carpet was littered with glass splinters. The intruder had left as he'd entered, reaching back through the broken pane and turning the key after him. It would have taken time to locate the safe let alone the key. And Rowlands wasn't a burglar. I couldn't see why anyone would have cut the bedroom phone and left the line to the study alive. Unless it was Jessica. She might even have been dying when I'd looked in on her.

I took the key out of the door and wiped it with my handkerchief. It was done before I realized the implication. You don't *have* to feel guilt. The urge to self-protection is instinctive. All you need is to know what others might think. And I knew only too well. I went back to the study. It's not easy to remember — I'm not sure what I'd have done at that moment, given the chance. The question was academic. Car doors slammed outside. I peeped from the window. A black Rover with a stubby radio mast sticking out of the roof was drawn up in front of the steps. The first man out was John Straight. The other four were unmistakably plainclothesmen. I opened the door for them. The last cop in closed it behind him carefully. Another drifted round behind me toward the kitchen. The man beside Straight had a Mongol face with wide padded cheekbones and eyes that were set forward. He turned them on me in a cursory inspection.

"This him?" he asked Straight. He wore a dirty trench coat and wilted felt hat that he tossed at a chair.

Straight nodded. He was unshaven, his face as expressionless as usual. A roll-necked sweater showed beneath his overcoat. The cop shifted his stance fractionally, his eyes restless.

"Detective-Superintendent Foster. I understand you found the body, Mr. Bain."

It registered that he already knew my name. Straight must have called the police immediately after hanging up on me.

"I found her," I admitted. "But not until this morning. She's upstairs but I think you'd better look in there first." I jerked my head towards the study.

"Why?" Foster wasted no time on the niceties.

I shrugged. "Because the house has been burgled, that's why." The words drifted away, leaving an echoing doubt. Straight's face was hostile with unspoken accusation.

"See what there is, Fletcher." Foster spoke to an aide. "And keep your eyes open for the Medical Officer — he should be here any moment. You said upstairs, Mr. Bain?" He was very close to me all the way up the stairs.

We filled the room, six of us, in a group round the bed. Foster grunted as he looked down at her.

"They never think about the mess they leave behind. Isn't there a maid?"

"She won't be here today," I said steadily. "Mrs. Straight told me to tell her not to come when I went out last night."

"I see," he mused. "So you were out last night." He kicked the length of telephone cord away from the wall and bent down between table and bed. He came up holding an empty glass on the end of his pencil. A ring of sediment clouded the bottom. He let the glass slide down on the table, right-side up.

"Ever seen this before?"

He was still talking to me. "No, I haven't," I said deliberately. "I was in here around seven, there was nothing. I'd have noticed."

His eyes darted everywhere. The interior fold in the lids gave them a swollen appearance.

"And that was the last time you saw her alive?" he inquired casually.

I shook my head. "I looked in when I got back. That would be just after nine. The lights were out. She was sleeping."

He glanced down at the tray on the floor. Nothing on it had been touched.

"How do you know?"

Each piece of dialogue seemed to wind a spring tighter. "I heard her breathing," I said.

"More likely dying," he said shortly and motioned at the bathroom. "You didn't look in there at all?"

I kept my temper. "Why would I?"

He smiled thinly. "To search for intruders." He poked the door back with his pencil. He came out of the bathroom holding a small bottle wrapped in his handkerchief. He put it down beside the glass. I recognized the brand name. They were the same pills she'd used the day before. Straight was sitting on a chair by the window. He averted his eyes as I looked at him. Suddenly I knew why. I hadn't mentioned the safe or the break-in when I'd called him. Yet he'd made sure I was in the house when the police arrived. I swung round to Foster.

"Could I have a word with you outside, Superintendent?"

He opened the bedroom door, positioning himself so that he was between me and the stairs. Light streamed through the window at the end of the corridor, brightening the bronze chrysanthemums Jessica had cut the day before. I lowered my voice.

"There's something you ought to know. She tried to kill herself yesterday with exactly the same pills."

He scraped the edge of his shoe over the carpet as if testing for dust.

"You think she had some more hidden away somewhere?"

He was just too offhand. "I don't think anything of the sort," I replied. "In fact I'd have known if she had. I called a doctor. He'll tell you the same as I do. That woman wanted to live."

He put his back against the wall and scratched away comfortably. "I understand you answered an advertisement for a companion. You seem to have come a long way in a couple of days."

I met his quizzical look squarely. "She was in trouble and I saved her life. Maybe the two things add up. Maybe I've come too far for a lot of people, Superintendent."

He winked at me. "Isn't there something else you wanted to tell me," he prompted. "Something about yourself?"

His tone was still casual but it was there in the padded eyes, the hostile stare of a thief-catcher sighting his quarry.

"What are you trying to prove?" I burst out. "You knew who I was when you walked in that door. So I told a lie to get this job. But I'm clean, don't you believe that?"

He moved his back off the wall. "I believe you told a lie to get the job," he said shortly.

A door slammed below. A man in a bowler hat, wearing a dark overcoat, ran up the stairs. He greeted Foster with brusque familiarity.

"You don't even let me finish breakfast now. Where is she?"

Foster pointed into the bedroom and touched my sleeve. The police surgeon gestured the men away from the bed. He bent down, sniffing the glass on the table. He took Jessica Straight's wrists in his hands, examining them carefully. He inspected the skin round her lips with a magnifying glass. Then he turned the body slightly, peering at the undersides of her arms. I saw the bruises, purple marks the size and shape of thumbs. My mouth went sour. I felt my heart banging my life away.

The police surgeon flicked a thermometer and inserted it under the dead woman's armpit. He took it out, speaking to Foster as if they were alone in the room.

"She's been dead about eight hours, an overdose of barbiturates. I wouldn't think she took it voluntarily. These labial lacerations, the multiple bruising on the arms, suggest the use of extreme external force. I'll know more when I've done a postmortem. You'd better call an ambulance." He tucked the thermometer in his waistcoat pocket.

Nobody looked at me — as if I already belonged to some higher authority. The doorbell rang violently. Foster's instruction was sharp.

"See who that is."

The cop at the window stuck his head out. I heard Martha's belligerent shout.

101

"What's happening? Open this door!"

Foster bellowed along the corridor. "Somebody let that woman in!" He was just out of sight, halfway between the bedroom and the stairs. It was now or never. I took two steps into the bathroom, turned the key, and flung the window wide. I went through it feet first, dragging the creeper with me as I dropped. My heels thudded into soft earth. I got up, forcing my way through the laurel bushes, out onto the driveway. Martha was already in the house. The police surgeon's Buick was parked near the gates. I covered the thirty yards at a dead run, bedlam breaking out behind me. I hurled myself into the driver's seat. The keys were in the dash. Foster's head appeared at an upstairs window as I switched on the motor. I put my foot down hard. The car shot forward as though kicked from behind. The offside door swung open, crashing against the gatepost. I dragged the wheel over, just missing a milk trolley coming up the hill. I grabbed one-handed at the door, driving like a maniac. My only thought was to put distance between myself and the house.

At the foot of the hill I turned east, joining the early morning traffic climbing up to Wimbledon Common. The signals on the crest were against me. Horse riders were cantering along a bridle path, a hundred yards away. A chauffeur-driven limousine drew up alongside. The driver looked over at the damaged door, pantomiming sympathy. I knew I had to ditch the Buick as soon as possible. Its description would be on the air by now. The first speed-cop I met, I was dead. The signals changed. I pulled off the highway onto the bridle path. The riders were a quarter of a mile ahead. The path ringed

102

the Common. There was no traffic, just a few people walking their dogs. I drove on slowly till the path curved through trees. There was no one in sight. I backed the Buick into the bushes and sprang out, leaving the keys. I trotted the quarter mile to the bus stop and took my place on the queue.

A bus swayed round the bend and stopped. We all shuffled forward as the Negro conductor counted his load.

I was last onto the platform. The upper deck was crowded with blank-faced office workers, miserable with cold. Coughing, smoking, rattling their newspapers. I dropped into an aisle seat and groped for change. The conductor pushed his way past the jutting knees. Eyes like chestnuts swimming in oil considered me curiously. I looked down, remembering that it was near November. I was wearing no overcoat. Green mold from the bushes streaked my jacket. There was mud on the bottoms of my trousers.

"Hammersmith Broadway."

He exchanged a ticket for the coin I offered. I used my handkerchief on my clothes. My passport was back in the house, together with Kirstie's home address and telephone number, the bundle of letters she'd sent to Elm Park Gardens. I lit a cigarette, borrowing a light from my neighbor. The deck was stacked against me — a pat hand dealt for Foster. All he had to do was sit back and play it. I'd saved Jessica Straight's life. Sure, they'd say — to establish her suicidal tendencies. The broken window in the drawing room — that had been me, too, trying to make it look like an outside job. I'd stayed on having planted the jewelry, hoping to bluff my way out. Then my nerve had gone and I'd run for it.

The man sitting next to me climbed over my legs. I moved into his seat, staring down through the steamed windows at the river beneath Putney Bridge. I kept seeing a man's back, strained with effort as he held Jessica by the arms, holding her till the drug he'd forced down her throat took effect. She'd been as good as dead when he left the bedroom. Suddenly I saw his face. It wasn't Jack the Rat. Rowlands was capable of anything but murder. *The face I saw was John Straight's.*

Behind that mask of sympathy lay a savage desire for revenge on a woman he blamed for his brother's death. He was as crazy as Mark must have been, watching with the same sort of twisted cunning, amused as we played the roles he'd written for us.

The bus halted with a jerk. Hammersmith Broadway. I ran down the stairs. It all added up but it was still no more than the inspired hunch of a man in deep trouble. And Foster had a better hunch of his own. I was a loner again with nowhere to go and only one person to help me, Kirstie. I crossed the road to the subway station and fed a coin into the ticket-vending machine. The track serving the eastbound trains was three-deep with passengers. We surged forward as a train rattled out of the tunnel. I shoved my way into a coach that was already overcrowded. The doors closed with a hiss. There was no need to grab at a hand strap. Pressure from the surrounding bodies held me upright.

I was back in a world of fear, like an animal that runs with the herd, sensing its selection for slaughter. I couldn't call Kirstie at home. Her phone would be tapped. There could well be a stakeout on her building, waiting for me to walk into the trap. Foster had all the pictures of me that he needed — mug-shots from prison, the photograph on my passport. He knew what I was wearing. In a few hours every prowl car in the city would be looking for me. My only hope was to get off the streets and find a refuge.

I fought my way from the train at Knightsbridge and walked through the tunnel to Sloane Street. There was a store selling men's clothing, thirty yards south. A snap-brim hat, quilt-lined mac, and a pair of gloves set me back fifteen pounds. I'd have to borrow money from Kirstie. I turned up Hans Crescent, sharp right into a real estate office. I closed the door behind me, entering into an atmosphere of hushed elegance. The room was furnished with period pieces. A thick carpet deadened my footsteps as I crossed to the desk by the window. I could hear typewriters clicking away in an adjoining office. A legend on the nearest desk identified the young man behind it. *Mr. P. Winearl.* He smiled as I pulled up a chair, fighting a bout of sneezing with his handkerchief. His hair and clothes were neat. Intelligent eyes were set in a roundish face. He tucked his handkerchief back in his sleeve.

"I'm sorry about that, sir. What can I do for you?"

I dropped my hat in my lap. "I'm looking for a furnished house to rent," I said easily. "For a year at least. It might be longer."

He turned his look into a brief and professional appraisal. "I see. And what sort of thing had you in mind, sir?"

A gilt-and-ormolu clock behind him said ten minutes to ten. Only a little while now and Kirstie would be at her office.

"Well," I said slowly. "It's got to be something large.

There are four of us — my wife and two children. But we must have room, no neighbors on top of us. I'm less concerned with how much I pay than with finding the right sort of place."

He nodded thoughtfully. "In London or outside, sir?"

"In London," I assured him. "Because of the children's school."

He pulled a batch of photographs from a drawer and spread them out in front of him. He flicked through till he'd narrowed his choice to three.

"I take it that you'll need four bedrooms at least, that sort of thing. That's no problem. What worries me is this question of space. It's what everyone's looking for and becoming harder and harder to find. Would you mind going out as far as Hampton Court for instance? I'm sorry, do you know London?"

Hampton Court was on the river, near enough to Kingston Hill to be dangerous, or near enough to be safe. It all depended how close to his chest Foster played his cards.

"I know where Hampton Court is." I reached for the photograph. It showed a half-timbered house with a gabled façade, a stretch of lawn in front of it. Trees appeared in the background. "Can you tell me something about this one?" I said.

He read the particulars from a typewritten slip. " 'Heron's Court. A riverside residence five hundred yards from the Palace and facing the Green. There are eight acres of gardens with fifty-feet moorings. It has six principal bedrooms, three modern bathrooms, a large drawing room and dining room, fully-fitted kitchen, central heating and two garages.' This property has never been let before, sir. As a matter of fact it belongs to a gentleman in the diplomatic service. He's just been posted to Karachi. I do know that the house is exceptionally well-furnished."

No neighbors, trees, and the river behind. I kept my voice casual. "What sort of rent are they asking?"

He sneezed again, apologizing from behind his handkerchief. He searched his list.

"Two thousand, five hundred pounds a year, sir. That's inclusive of rates and taxes but not the public services. The owner wouldn't want to let it for more than a year."

I nodded, picking the picture up again. "We're not even sure that we'd want to stay longer than that, anyway. When could we look the place over? Naturally I'd like my wife to be here. She's in Paris at the moment. I'm expecting her back on Saturday."

He glanced at the calendar. "That only gives us two days. The thing is, this house has only just come on the books. We're not really supposed to be negotiating till the owner's sister has cleared out their personal effects. And she's in Scotland for two weeks. How soon would you want to move in? That's assuming you like the place, of course."

I shrugged. "We're not in that much of a hurry, Mr. Winearl. But we would like to see round as soon as possible. I don't have that much time to look for a house. Isn't there a gardener or someone on the premises?"

He shook his head regretfully. "I'm afraid not. It's just one of those things. Mr. Marlow has got rid of all his staff. You'd be starting from scratch. We could give you the names of some reputable agencies. We don't work on Saturdays

107

but I could show you round on Monday if that would do?"

I made a show of hesitation before answering. "Monday's good. How about eleven o'clock, here?"

He made a note in his appointment book. "And the name is?"

"Bernard Brady." It was as good as another.

"Then I'll expect you at eleven on Monday, Mr. Brady." He came to his feet courteously as I picked up my hat. "There's just one thing. The house might be in disorder. As I told you, I can't contact the owner's sister till she gets back from Edinburgh. We don't have her address there."

"Don't worry about that," I smiled. "If we like the place, I'll give you my check and references there and then. That'll save some time. Thanks for your help."

"Thank *you*, Mr. Brady." He watched, still standing as I walked out, step one of my plan for survival completed.

My next stop was a few yards round the corner, an optician's on Brompton Road. I bought a pair of glare-proof glasses with tinted lens. From the phone booth on the other side of the road I counted four men wearing the same sort of mac and hat. I called Kirstie's office, disguising my voice. I gave the name of an account that I knew she handled. There was no need to ask if the police had been in contact with her. Her voice told me.

"It's Collins," I said carefully. "Phillips Fine Foods. I was wondering whether you could see me later today. It's about the script on the new commercial. The trouble is I'm tied up till later."

She coughed guardedly. I guessed that someone was in the room with her.

"I think so," she answered. "I suppose you know that the market research people have been after me for information?"

I had the booth door open, holding it with my foot, watching for anything that looked like a police car.

"I imagined they would," I said. "I'll tell you all about it. Could you make it about eight? Somewhere in the West End would be best for me. Is Kelly's OK?"

The name would mean nothing to anyone else. The small members club was on Hamilton Place, opposite the Dorchester. Kelly was the woman who worked behind the bar.

She hesitated fractionally. "I might be a little late. I'm supposed to be meeting the research people again at seven. It's you they'd really like to talk to, of course."

I had no doubt about it. "They'll have to wait," I said. "Stall them. I need time. I'll see you at eight, then."

I dropped the receiver on the rest and walked out of the booth. There was no sign of a police car. Nobody stepping out of a doorway, with suddenly lowered newspaper. The chances were that Foster didn't yet know where Kirstie worked. Maybe he hadn't even asked her. He'd handle her carefully at first. But as soon as he made up his mind which side she was on, someone would follow wherever she went. I could show her how to beat a tail, sure. But it had to be done in a way that left her in the clear. When the police lost her, they had to believe it was because of their own stupidity.

It was almost eleven. I wasted a few minutes in a coffee bar planning my next move. The moves *had* to be planned now. If the breaks kept running with me, I could count on four days' shelter. Four days to translate a hunch into facts that a hardnosed cop would accept. I paid my check and ducked into the subway again. I surfaced at King's Cross, glad of the warm lining in my mac. The east wind was merciless. I walked north into the mean streets behind the railroad terminal. Dingy houses bore dubious cards in the windows. The blocks of cheap stores displayed flashy clothing, marked-down canned goods and Japanese transistors. The place I was looking for was a two-story building set back by the railroad lines. Iron railings protected dank weeds growing up through cinders. A board screwed to the outside wall read

ALOYSIUS HICKEY LIMITED, TOY MANUFACTURERS.

I turned the handle. The door led directly into a cement-floored factory. Girls with their heads wrapped in scarves were feeding strip metal into power presses. Others were at benches, assembling plastic space helmets. The whole place stank of petroleum-based adhesive. The noise of the machinery was deafening. A swing door on my right led through to a passage. I followed a series of arrows, round a bend and up a flight of stone stairs.

The man sitting in the office was reading the *Sporting Life*, his forehead corrugated with concentration. One lank strand of hair was plastered over his scalp unconvincingly. He was wearing a checked jacket, a dirty gray shirt and a tie with a large Windsor knot. He put the race sheet down, holding his place with a finger and nodding like a Chinese image. His eyes were like a bird's, unwinking, the pupils ringed with white. It was three years since I'd seen him but he didn't seem surprised. Not that I'd expected it. If I'd walked in wearing two heads the odds were that he'd have greeted me with the

110

same deadpan expression. The first thing he did after inspecting me carefully was close all the drawers in his desk and turn his correspondence face down.

The air shimmered over an oil-fired heater. I cleared a chair of a pair of race glasses and sat down.

"Long time no see, Professor. How's the toy dodge?"

His brogue was as thick as the day he'd left Mullingar. "I'm losing money, Macbeth. Losing money."

There was a tray on the desk with a metal teapot and a cup. He poured himself some of the lukewarm brew.

"And the horses?" I asked. Protocol had to be satisfied.

"Things is bad all round," he said sadly. "It's the certainties that's ruining me. And how is it with you, Macbeth?"

I could feel his toes curling in his shoes at the prospect of a touch.

"They could be better," I admitted. I took a cigarette from the packet on the desk.

"Isn't it the truth," he sighed and put the pack in his pocket. There was a long silence during which we both contemplated the next piece of dialogue. The Professor was deeply mistrustful of human nature, his own included. Rumor had it that he'd once worked for a firm of safe manufacturers, that he'd gambled himself into the hands of a Battersea bookmaker. The story went on that he'd paid off his debt with the secrets of a strong room in a city bank. True or false, he'd been introduced to me as a sort of general supplier to the fraternity. There was little in the way of larcenous equipment that Hickey couldn't provide given time and his price. Skeleton keys, telescopic ladders, oxygen tanks, plastic explosives. Nobody knew where his supplies came from. He chose his customers carefully and his methods of delivery were devious. The one attempt by the law to put him inside had backfired. Hickey had been acquitted and the police had been lumbered with a suit for wrongful arrest. He'd won damages. Since then they'd left him severely alone. He lived by himself in a flat across the landing, surrounded by old cuttings of crime reports, form books, and forgotten cups of tea. If he drank any other sort of liquid, nobody had heard about it.

I put his mind at rest. "This isn't a touch, Professor. I need a set of keys."

"Keys, is it?" he said more comfortably. "That's not what I've been hearing, at all. Whispers from the fashionable part of town. That you're in a fair line of business and behaving yourself. Selling travel to the upper classes. Is there no truth in it?"

I shook my head. "Just a vicious rumor. I need a gun, too."

He turned sharply, facing the window as if he expected to see the Police Commissioner's head appear there.

"Their ears get longer by the hour," he said darkly. "And the noses on them sharper. I get twitches, Macbeth, about the time when they're putting the cell lights out and the lads is dreaming of home."

I looked at him steadily. "So do I. That's why I'm here. I've got to have your help, Hickey." It was as much as I dared say. Believing that honor existed among thieves was a sure way to get clobbered.

His blank bird stare fixed me. "I always liked you, Macbeth, for the head that's on you. You were never one for the violence."

I loosened my coat. The room was stuffy. "I'm still not. This is insurance. I need a gun and a full set of keys. Do I get them or not?"

He picked up his race glasses, focusing through the window and panning along the street.

"I'm off to Sandown, Macbeth. You've chosen the wrong time."

I held the butt in the tray till the ash burned my thumb. "*Look* at me, Hickey," I pleaded. "Can't you see I'm in trouble?"

He did look at me. It seemed an age before he made his mind up. "How soon do you need them?" he asked finally.

"*Now*," I replied. "I'll find whatever money you're asking."

He put his binoculars down, spreading his hands over the top of the heater.

"I never took a shotgun to a man in trouble. We'll not talk about money now. I know you well. You'll be back in your own good time, isn't it right?"

I breathed easier. "I'll be back," I promised.

He showed a mouthful of long, stained teeth. "With a present for a friend in need. Here's what you do. It's almost twelve. Get yourself a cup of tea. Any time after one, you'll go to the Left Luggage office at St. Pancras Station. There'll be a bag there waiting for you. You'll not need a ticket. Just say you're Mr. Brown. Have you got that, now — Mr. Brown, Left Luggage, St. Pancras?"

I buttoned my coat and stood up. "I won't forget you, Hickey."

"You won't indeed," he said smiling again. "And good

luck to you! Now go out the back way. They'll not see you through the windows."

I left through an empty yard, coming out under the railroad arches. It was a brand new ball game and I was in it. I had a meal in a sleazy café on Euston Road. The big clock in the concourse said ten past one as I walked into the station. I had no doubt that the bag would be there. Hickey took his word seriously. I made my claim, retrieving a small canvas holdall.

I traveled to Hampton Court by train and bus. Heron's Court wasn't difficult to locate. The name was attached to a high wooden fence near the gate. I walked on, getting a glimpse of grass in front of the house. Beeches backed the fence, screening the gardens from the road. Fifty yards distant, a second gate opened onto a back driveway. I dropped the bag, bent down, and retied my shoelace. There was nobody near but a woman pushing a pram in the opposite direction. I unlatched the gate. The driveway curved round between the trees to a couple of brick garages. Grass sloped down to a boathouse. There was a towpath on the opposite bank of the river, thick bushes behind it. The trees enclosed the property in absolute privacy.

The flimsy door on the boathouse was unlocked. A plank floor inside went halfway across the width of the building. An electric dinghy bobbed gently at its edge. I lowered myself into it. The batteries were flat. An oar floated in the bilge water in the bottom of the boat. I climbed out and put the bag on a mildewed wicker table. There was a clear view of the rear of the house through the window. The style was Tudor with timber-and-plaster exterior and leaded windows. The brick staff wing was an obvious addition. The best place for me to hit was the back door. I'd be hidden from road and river. Once inside, all I had to worry about was the chance caller. The odds were against it. The place had been unoccupied for a month, the owner's sister safe in Scotland.

I unzipped the holdall. Inside was a plastic bag wrapped in old newspaper. The package held two key rings, a pair of long-nosed pliers and an automatic pistol. The trousseau of keys differed from the ordinary in two ways. There were no stops on the finely-tooled shanks. The patterns cut in the wards were basic. There were none of the useless indentations designed to impress the layman. With these in my hands I could beat nine out of ten mortise locks. I checked the clip in the gun — loaded. The weapon was a five-shot twenty-two, Spanish-made. The metal was scarred where a file had been used to remove the numbers. I took out the plug of chewing gum sealing the end of the barrel. The gun fitted comfortably in my hip pocket, inconspicuous under my jacket.

I crossed the grass to the staff wing. The kitchen curtains were drawn. The back door hung square and solid, not a crack between it and the frame. I pushed my shoulder against it, gauging the resisting pressure. If there were bolts, they hadn't been used. But the key had been left in the lock inside. The tip just showed. I took the pliers in my gloved hands and clamped the barreled ends round the tip of the key. I turned my wrists in a clockwise direction. The pliers slipped. There wasn't enough purchase. I took a fresh grip, stopping with the key in an upright position. I jiggled it back gently till the pliers were well into the lock. I heard the key fall on the floor inside.

I selected a dropped-E skeleton. There wasn't enough lift.

The third choice gave me the right feel. The levers turned over. I nudged the door with my knee. It swung inwards. I stepped forward quickly, picked the house key from the floor and used it to relock the door. The kitchen was modern with a composition floor and bright yellow walls. The faucet in the sink ran water. The light switch worked. The first door I opened led to a servants' sitting room. There were chintz-covered armchairs, a television set and a Welsh dresser with pewter pots hanging from it. I went into the adjoining room. Blankets and sheets were stacked on the twin beds. The curtains were drawn. I walked out to a hall gloomy with oak and suits of armor. A couple of letters lay on the tray. Both were postmarked nine days previously. The dining room and drawing room were shrouded in dustsheets. Tags under the portraits on the walls dated them back to the seventeenth century. There were some early English watercolors, Georgian silver, a vast clock in a walnut case.

I ran up the broad stairway. Every inch of floor was carpeted, including the bathrooms. The water was heated electrically. I peeped into a bedroom. I could see now why the agent had questioned the state of the place. It looked as if the owners had stopped halfway through packing. Dresses and furs were strewn over a shell-shaped bed. The adjoining bathroom was pink-tiled. Glass apothecary bottles were filled with colored bath salts. A faint scent lingered as if a woman had just stepped out of the sunken tub.

Through another door was a man's dressing room. Half a dozen suits and a couple of overcoats still hung in the closet. A set of car keys pinned down a large envelope on top of the tallboy. I opened the envelope. Inside was a driving license, an insurance policy, a couple of charge cards, and a folded sheet of writing paper. I read it.

Dear Margot,

Sorry to leave you with all this mess to take care of. As I told you on the phone, the last-minute rush was hectic. We literally didn't have time to do more than we did.

Laura says not to worry about her things — moth-proof bags or whatever — I'm leaving the keys of the car herewith. As soon as you're back from Scotland, phone Hayley's Garage. Kensington 1387. They'll collect.

> Hasty love,
> Richard

The name was the same as that on the documents. Richard Marlow.

I tried a double-breasted suit for size. The jacket was passable, the waistband of the trousers an inch too big. I kept the suit on, transferring the things from my own pockets. Nothing I was wearing now, except my shoes, corresponded with the description the police had of my clothes. I picked up the car keys and documents and went downstairs. There was a board in the kitchen with more keys. Each of them bore a tag. One read GARAGE. I unfastened the back door and walked up to the brick building.

As soon as I entered the garage I knew I'd hit the jackpot. The chrome on a Mark Ten Jaguar glittered in the semi-darkness. I checked the tires, oil, and battery. All were in order. I went into the house again and brought my old clothes down to the servant's bedroom. This was going to be my base. At the first sign of danger I could break for the back door, the trees or the river. I looked round for food. All I found were a few cans of fruit. The refrigerator was empty. I'd have to stock up.

I made one of the beds and sat down. All the curtains were drawn on the lower floor. No one on the outside could see in. It was only four o'clock. Four more hours till I met Kirstie. The next thing I had to do was reach Pardoe. I'd located three phones in the house, two upstairs, one down. But I didn't dare risk using any of them. I'd noticed a booth near the bridge. I put my hat and coat on, meeting my reflection in the mirror. The tinted glasses were a doubtful touch in late October. I could only hope that people would think I had eye trouble. I went out through the back door, taking the key with me. Mist was coming off the river. It was already twilight. The trees afforded cover to the gate. There was no one there to see me slip out to the road.

The booth by the bridge was empty. I stepped in and dialed Pardoe's number. His integrity seemed the one sure thing in a nightmare of doubt and betrayal. I hung up, suddenly afraid. What *could* he do for me? I was on the run for murder, asking the victim's lawyer to listen to an accusation I couldn't prove. I forced myself to dial again. He *had* to listen.

"Police," I told the girl. "I want to talk to Mr. Pardoe."

Her voice was muffled as she spoke into the intercom box. Then Pardoe, quietly assured.

"This is Edward Pardoe."

I had the booth door open ready to move. "It's Bain. You've got to help me. I didn't touch her, Pardoe. Straight's framing me."

I could hear him breathing heavily. Then the line went dead. I hurried out of the booth, along the tree-lined road and through the gate. Something was wrong. It wasn't his refusal to answer — fair enough to have no truck with a man wanted by the police. Something had happened to him in the five-seconds' pause after I'd spoken. I was as certain of it as though I'd been there in the room with him. And I knew why instinctively. It was the mention of Straight's name. It was a hunch again but it left me in no doubt. The clue to Pardoe's concern was the clue to the frame-up.

I backed the Jaguar out of the garage, drove to the road without lights, and shut the gate behind me. I wasn't worried about neighbors. The nearest house was two hundred yards away. The powerful car handled smoothly. I beat the evening rush and parked on the corner of King's Bench Walk. There was no sign of Pardoe's Bentley. I stood in a doorway, watching his office. Five o'clock. One light after another went out. Three girls chattered down the steps, separating at the top of the street. The sound of their heels faded. A man called good night from a neighboring doorway. I slipped out and ducked into Pardoe's porch. The street door was open, the light still burning in the hall. The office lock was a simple mortise. I turned it off with one of Hickey's keys. A match flame guided me into Pardoe's room. I negotiated the furniture, feeling my way round to the cupboards. The shotgun Pardoe had shown me lay in a canvas case on the floor. The lettered shelves above it were crammed with folders. I searched quickly under S. If the Straight file was kept there, it was missing now. The safe in the corner mocked me. I was standing at the desk when headlights lit the room. I dropped to the floor as a car stopped outside. I crawled on hands and knees to the nearest door. There was nothing in the tiny cloakroom but a basin and some hooks. No windows — no

119

other way out. I pulled the door shut and stood with my ear against it.

Footsteps echoed in the outer office. A crack of light appeared at the bottom of the door. I heard Pardoe clear his throat. The chair creaked behind his desk. Then a bell tinkled as he lifted the phone from its rest. I pulled the gun out of my pocket. I couldn't remember whether I'd shut the cupboard doors. I imagined him sitting there smiling, quietly dialing the police as he looked across at the cloakroom door. Suddenly his voice was hoarse with anger.

"Of course it's me. I've been trying to reach you all day!"

I heard him shift in his chair, waiting for an answer. He cut in again, demolishing whatever reply was given.

"Ever since this morning! You must be out of your mind. I've taken all I can but this time you've gone too far. This is murder. No it *isn't* the time to discuss things. I've got to think. I'll call you later."

The phone bell tinkled again. I heard the jingle of keys, the safe being opened and shut. He'd used no name but I knew he'd been talking to Straight. The lights went out. I was one door behind him all the way to the street.

I hid in the porch, watching him cross the road to his car. He passed the Jaguar without giving it a second glance. He bent down at the rear of the Bentley, looking back over his shoulder. Then he unlocked the trunk and put a briefcase inside. I had the Jaguar moving as his taillights vanished towards the Embankment. I kept a couple of cars between us all the way up Northumberland Avenue. Just before we reached the signals at Trafalgar Square, he swerved onto the inside lane. I knew where he lived, an apartment building off Belgrave Square. I gambled that he was heading there.

The lights changed. The Bentley slid forward into the Mall. I drove on his lights as far as the Palace, gunned past him round the monument and caught the next set of signals on the amber. I looked back in the rear-view mirror. The Bentley was trapped by the red. I made a right turn into Belgravia, crossed the square and drove onto the forecourt of the German Embassy. I left the Jaguar there and hurried round the corner into Chesham Place.

A car ramp sloped down by the side of the lighted portico. I walked down the narrow strip of pavement to the underground garage. There was no attendant, nothing but a line of empty cars parked in stenciled bays. An elevator served the apartments. I stationed myself behind a pillar and waited, eyes on the top of the ramp. Five minutes passed then the front end of the Bentley nosed its way gently down. The sound of the motor echoed from the vaulted ceiling. I broke cover as Pardoe maneuvered into a slot near the elevator.

He killed the motor, reaching for his hat as I wrenched the door open. I was in the seat beside him before he knew what had happened.

I showed him the gun, speaking with difficulty. "Get this thing up the ramp again."

His fingers stiffened on the wheel, his eyes flicking toward the elevator gates. I saw him assessing the chances of a quick dash for them.

"Don't try it," I warned grimly.

He swallowed hard, chicken-necked and hoarse. "You don't think you'll get away with this, do you?"

"I'm going to try," I said savagely and dug the barrel of the gun hard into his body.

He winced, turning the ignition key. The Bentley purred

121

up to the street. Pardoe looked left and right as we crossed the sidewalk. A porter peered out from the entrance. I was sitting sideways, smiling at Pardoe, the gun concealed beneath my hat.

"Right," I ordered.

His head came round slowly. His eyes challenged me. For a second I thought I'd lost him. All he had to do was sit tight, the big car halfway out on the street. A man was mailing a letter in the box across the way. The porter was still watching us from the portico. A shout would bring either of them.

Then Pardoe spoke. "Let's talk this over before you do too much damage. I can help you."

Half an hour before I'd have bought it. Not anymore. "Get going," I warned.

He shrugged and touched the accelerator, gray head erect and imposing, the proconsul facing the mob. I sat tense as he wheeled in front of a cab, relaxing when his speed slackened. He drove carefully, obeying my instructions. I watched for the first false move. He was a long way from beaten.

It was past six when we reached Hampton Court. I let him pass the house, making him turn on the Green. Staggered street lights showed a patchwork of deserted sidewalk. I turned the headlights off.

"Straight ahead," I ordered. "I'll tell you when to stop." Mist came to meet us on the driveway, rolling up from the river, drifting round the half-hidden house. I yanked the keys out of the dash and put them in my pocket. I nudged him out with the gun.

"Down the path."

I locked the kitchen door behind us, shoving him in front

of me into the hall. I wasn't risking taking him out again. The phones here were automatic. There'd be no record of local calls. I leaned back against the paneling, watching him in the half-light. It was too dark to see his expression.

"You'd better listen to me," I said. "We're alone in this house. I don't have to tell you what that means. Now you're going to pick up that phone and speak to your wife. Tell her you've been called out of town for a couple of days on business. If she's not there leave a message. And make it sound credible."

I saw his shoulders move. His voice was hesitant. "What do you want, money?"

"I want you to do as you're told," I answered. "What's the number?"

He gave it to me. I struck a match and dialed. As soon as I heard the ringing tone, I stuck the receiver in his hand, holding the gun behind his ear.

Long training kept his voice sounding normal. "Kathy? I've been trying to get hold of you. I won't be home tonight. In fact it doesn't look as if I'll be back till Saturday. No, Birmingham. I *can't* send anyone else, dear. Yes, I'll phone as soon as I'm sure. Good night, dear. Good night."

I took the phone from him quickly. A cord hung from the velvet curtains over the front door. I pulled it out. There was a box of candles in a kitchen drawer. I stuck one in a saucer and lit it. I pointed at the door in front of us. His face was apprehensive in the waxing flame. The cord in my hand seemed to worry him. I shoved him again, this time to the bed nearer the window. He looked up with a sort of defiant courage.

"What do you intend to do — kill me, too?"

"There's killing and killing," I said. "I'd sooner be dead than rot in jail for the rest of my life. That's what you're trying to do to me."

He took a deep breath. "I think you're a sick man, a very sick man. You need help."

It was beautifully done, the struggle to be compassionate as if belief in my guilt was tinged with understanding. But it was false. I didn't want him to know yet how close I was to him.

"Roll over on your stomach," I said savagely. "Hands behind your back."

He shrugged and obeyed me. I corded his wrists to his ankles, turned him on his side and stuck a pillow under his head. Then I folded a sheet lengthwise, passing it over his body so that the ends dangled on the floor. I knotted them under the bed, making a rough kind of straight-jacket. He was in good shape for a man of his age but he stood no chance of getting out of there. I ripped the pillow slip in two.

"Open your mouth."

I was careful with my fingers, gagging him with the rest of the slip. I threw a couple of blankets over him and shut the door. He could still breathe through his nose. Mist hung in the trees outside. The only sound was that of water slapping against the boathouse. I walked up the path to the Bentley and took the briefcase from the trunk.

There are moments that memory retains, every sensory impression indelibly recorded. I can remember sitting down at the kitchen table, the silence of the house, the way the candle burned lopsidedly, the smell of the river creeping under the door. I emptied the briefcase onto the table. I spread the documents out on the checked cloth. The first was impressive with scrolled lettering, tape, and red sealing wax. It was a Deed of Trust in favor of John de Gruchy Straight.

I read it through twice before the legal jargon made sense. A quarter of a million pounds was at stake, most of it vested in blue chip holdings. Straight's inheritance of the sum was based on a single clause that finished:

". . . and that two doctors qualified in the United Kingdom and licensed in the practice of psychiatry shall examine and determine the sanity of the said John de Gruchy Straight at any time prior to his fortieth birthday . . ."

Failing this, provision was made for his keep for life in an institution approved by the trustees. In which case the bulk of the fortune passed to the League for Cancer Research. The trustees were Pardoe and a firm of merchant bankers. A certificate was attached to the Deed. It was signed by two doctors, dated the twelfth of August 1967, and testified that upon examination they found John de Gruchy Straight to be legally sane.

I picked up a bunch of canceled checks. Each was payable to Bramwell Grange Remedial Home. Each had a receipt stapled to it. The first date was December 1950, the last March 1967. This meant that Straight had been under restraint for seventeen years. For "Remedial Home" read "Mental Asylum," I thought.

There was one separate check and receipt made out in the name of the Hayley Memorial Clinic. This was dated 9 August 1967: *For professional services, two thousand, one hundred guineas.*

All the checks had been signed by Pardoe. My first wave of hope receded. I was sure that to prove my innocence I had to prove Straight's guilt. There was nothing in any of this that the police would accept as conclusive — not one single fact that would get me off the hook. And time was running out.

The more I thought about it, the more certain I became that Pardoe was shielding an accomplice, not a friend or client. I put the documents back in the briefcase and blew the candle out. Then I locked up and walked out to Pardoe's car. I put it away in the garage. It took me over an hour to get to Sloane Street. I bought a carton of groceries at a late-night neighborhood store at the end of Kinnerton Street. A slim pencil flashlight caught my eye. I added it to my purchases — bread, milk, sugar, tea, a few cans of meat and fish. I carried the carton out to the street, one more pedestrian in the raw October night. The windows of the German Embassy were in darkness, the gates leading to the forecourt shut but not locked. I opened them quietly and walked over to the Jaguar. A card was tucked under one of the windshield wipers. A message was penciled on it. EMBASSY OF THE FEDERAL REPUBLIC OF GERMANY CONSULAR SECTION. *This space is private property. Please refrain from trespassing on it.*

I drove out as quietly as I could, not bothering to shut the gates after me. The place I wanted was on Hamilton Place, opposite the Dorchester Hotel. I left the Jaguar outside and ran down the steps. The club was no different from twenty others in the neighborhood. A small basement room with tables and bar, fuzzy lighting and taped background music. A man and woman were talking to the fat blonde in front of the mirrored bottles. She broke off, recognizing me. After a

126

minute she smiled. But without any meaning. Kelly had disapproved of me for years. I bought myself a drink and took it to the far end of the room. I put the briefcase underneath the table and settled down to watch the entrance. Time dragged on. Eight o'clock. Twenty past. Suddenly the door opened. Kirstie came in, her small anxious face framed in dark hair. She looked pale and worried.

I waved, standing up to catch her attention. I held her tightly in my arms, whispering.

"She's got her eye on us. Careful."

I pulled a chair for her and walked across to the bar. "A man-size drink for a woman. Gin and tonic."

She held a glass under the upturned bottle of Beefeater. "What are you doing to that girl?" she asked sourly.

I poured tonic water over the ice cubes. "Nothing that needs your attention."

"Men," she sniffed, her mouth tight with disapproval. "I don't know why we bother with you."

I carried the drink back to the table and bent over Kirstie, undoing her green tailored coat.

"Are you sure you weren't followed?" I asked quietly.

She nodded, holding the glass in both hands. Her fingers were unsteady.

"Come on, drink it," I urged.

She did her best then put the glass down. Her eyes filled with tears. She groped in her handbag, passing me a folded piece of newspaper. The report had been torn from the *Evening Standard*.

WOMAN FOUND DEAD IN BED

An emergency call early this morning sent police racing to an address in the Kingston Hill district. They found Mrs. Jessica

Straight dead in an upstairs room in her luxury home. Mrs. Straight, an attractive widow of 36, had lived in the house for the past eleven years. A spokesman for the police said that preliminary investigations had established the cause of death as an overdose of barbiturate pills. Foul play is suspected. Detectives searched the West End later today looking for a man thought to be able to help in their enquiries.

The stock phrasing was sinister. I stuffed the paper in my pocket and stood.

"Let's get out of here. And try to act normally."

She came to her feet, smiling shakily. Kelly leaned over the bar, the bracelets rattling up her fat arm as she leveled it at me.

"I know him of old, dear. He's a monster. Don't let him bully you."

Somebody laughed as we went up the steps. Kirstie's eyes were fearful as I pushed her into the Jaguar. I drove into the park and along the South Carriageway. I stopped behind the barracks and switched off the motor.

"OK, what happened with the police?"

She grabbed my hand as if its possession meant more than words. "They came to the flat, two of them. Just as I was going to work. One was a Superintendent. He said his name was Foster. He asked me a lot of questions about you."

"Sure," I answered. "When you'd last seen me, who my friends were, whether I'd given you anything to keep for me — like Mrs. Straight's jewelry."

She moved her head miserably. "He asked me if I knew that you'd been that woman's lover."

I wasn't surprised. The rules went, once they'd decided on

128

action. They bit, butted, and kneed whoever they could get their hands on.

"The oldest gag in the book and you fall for it," I said bitterly.

She shook me roughly. "Even if it had been true it wouldn't have mattered. I love you."

"I suppose you told him that too?"

"Yes, I did," she answered defiantly. "But that's all I did tell him. I could have said that whatever happens I'm on your side. They kept me nearly an hour at Scotland Yard. You know what that's like. Those corridors, the doors opening behind as you go, heads looking out. And Foster just sitting there waiting. He wasn't vicious or threatening. He just asked questions and listened, as if he was certain I'd give you away if he kept on long enough."

"He's dead right at that," I replied. It was dark and lonely under the trees beyond the street lamps. "You might as well know the rest. I've got Pardoe, tied to a bed in Hampton Court."

Her face was aghast. "My God," she said heavily.

"My God," I repeated and opened the briefcase. "I was in his office tonight. He took these out of his safe." I told her of the phone call, the drive at gunpoint.

She held the documents under the dash light, then gave them back to me, her voice puzzled.

"I don't understand. Only psychopaths kill without reason, surely. These doctors say he's sane."

I put the papers away. "Doctors make mistakes. How do we know who they are, anyway?"

She looked at me sadly. "But the trustees would. Can't

129

you see, darling? We *have* to go to the police now. I'm coming with you."

I couldn't bring myself to blame her for dreaming of a father figure holding up traffic for little old ladies.

"The script doesn't go like that," I said quietly. "They're not boy scouts, they're cops. And they're going to pin this thing on *me*, Kirstie."

Her face was obstinate. "I don't believe it. Give me a cigarette." Her face was even sadder in the match flame. "Do you trust me?"

"I love you," I answered.

She took my hand again. "Then listen to me, *please!* We've got to telephone Superintendent Foster. He gave me a number. If he's not there, they'll tell us where he'll be. He'll help us, I'm sure of it."

I shrugged resignedly, switching on the motor. "One thing's obvious to me. I should never have involved you in any of this, Kirstie. You've got to cut out while there's still time. I'll drive you to the station. You don't need a bag. Take the first train down to your parents. And stay there."

She drooped, the cigarette burning unheeded in her fingers. When she finally did speak, each word was an endearment.

"But I *am* involved. For better or for worse. Whatever happens, I'm not leaving you." She laid her cheek against mine, her touch fiercely possessive.

I drove down Queen's Gate and stopped in front of the post office. One of the phone booths was unoccupied.

"Give me Foster's number," I said.

She gave me a card from her handbag. I took it into the booth. As soon as the voice answered, I recognized it. I tried to speak but the words wouldn't come.

"Foster," he repeated, this time more sharply.

I put the phone down, walked back to the car and climbed in beside her.

"I can't do it," I said. "I'm scared. I just can't do it."

She dug her hands deep in her coat pockets. "It's funny. I don't know why but I keep thinking of you stepping through that little door, a free man. I remember your face on the train, the way you smelled the coffee at breakfast. A new world, you said. What happened to us?"

My chin dropped on my chest. "Don't you think I haven't asked myself the same question? Ten months of it, trying to play their rules — *your* rules, Kirstie."

"I know," she said in a low voice. "And you blame me, don't you? How do you suppose I felt knowing that, hearing Foster talk about you as if you were some kind of vicious animal? 'A man on the run isn't human any longer. He'll stop at nothing.' That's what he said."

None of it changed a thing. Injustice, frustration. The fence was still there with me on the outside. And even she couldn't see it.

"And I'm proving him right, is that what you're trying to tell me? So what comes next?"

"I don't know," she said despairingly. "But I'm here and you're my responsibility."

Cars flicked by, the faces of the people happy and animated. But I ran in an ever-narrowing circle with Foster waiting in the center.

"What do you think'll happen to me if I give myself up?"

Her voice was hesitant. "You're only making things worse. I can't *think* the way you do. All my life I've believed in right and wrong. Foster said something else. 'If you care for this

131

man, pray! Pray that he gets some sense in his head before it's too late.' "

"Too late for *what?*" I asked bitterly. "To put me in a cell with no chance to defend myself? He thinks I'm guilty. He'll use you or anyone else to get his hands on me."

I felt her shiver. "I didn't think I'd ever be able to say this. But right or wrong doesn't matter anymore. I'll do whatever you want me to do. Just tell me."

The bad decision for the good motive. That's how far I'd driven her. Maybe Foster had something — a man on the run ceased to be human. But there was nothing I could do about it. My course was set.

"I need time, darling," I said. "Time to get proof and you can help me. I'm not kidding myself about Pardoe anymore. He won't talk. I've got to go back to the beginning. I'm going down to this Home in the morning. Get hold of your doctor tonight. See if he knows anything about the people who signed this sanity certificate. Ask him about the Hayley Memorial Clinic."

Her voice was unsteady. "I don't want to leave you, Macbeth. I don't seem to be able to even think anymore. It was hopeless at the office today. Brice noticed it. He wanted me to go home."

I turned her face toward me. "Listen to me. From now on we've got to be doubly careful. Tonight doesn't mean a thing. It's only a matter of time before Foster puts someone on your tail. And we've got to be able to meet."

She blinked hard, wet eyes staring into mine. "Where?"

I thought for a moment. "That hairdresser you go to on Dover Street. I seem to remember a back entrance."

132

She nodded. "There are two. One goes right through to the boutique in Albermarle Street."

"Then go there at half past twelve," I said. "Tell the girl you want an appointment some time next week. If you *are* being tailed, they won't know about the Albermarle Street exit. And they won't come into the place with you. Call a cab from the boutique. I'll be at the main entrance to the zoo at one o'clock. If you don't see me, *wait.* I won't be far away."

She dried her eyes determinedly. "One o'clock."

I put the car in gear and drove along Brompton Road to the cab stand. I opened the door for her.

"Good night, darling, and have faith."

She did her best to smile. I watched her pick her way through the swirl of traffic. The meter flag went down on the leading cab. Part of me seemed to vanish with its taillights. I made a left turn and headed back west. I was halfway across Hampton Court Bridge when I noticed the two men standing near the bus shelter. My stomach tightened involuntarily. No question what they were. The strategic choice of position, just out of the light, eyes searching the shadows for the first suspect walking a little too quickly. They wouldn't be looking for me, specifically, but I put my foot down hard as I turned the corner. I drove through the gates and put the Jaguar in the garage next to the Bentley. The temperature outside had dropped sharply. The grass was ghostly with frost. The mournful sound of church bells floated across the water, dragging me back in time to a night thirty years ago. A farmhouse on the edge of a Saskatchewan village. Church bells had been ringing then. I'd crept out through the barn,

133

running away from home for the first time. I remembered the sweet smell of the cattle, my pony's nickering. Then my grandfather had walked out of the snow-heavy spruce trees, tall in the twilight. God, in a fur hat and a mackinaw — all-knowing, all-powerful.

I picked up the carton of groceries. Moor hens were rustling in the reeds by the boathouse. Everything else was quiet. I put the carton on the kitchen table, knowing that the feeling of relief wouldn't last. I lit the candle and took it into the bedroom. Pardoe was in the same position, the gag soaked with spittle. I untied him. He sat up, rubbing his wrists and ankles. The gag had left weals across his florid cheeks. I looked at him from behind the gun.

"Someone killed a defenseless woman last night. Someone who knew how long I was going to be out, that I had a police record."

He didn't even answer. "It could only have been one person," I added.

His mouth was like a trap. "God knows what you can hope to get out of all this."

The way he said it made me want to take him by the throat. "You bastard," I said. "Straight killed her and you know it!"

"I know you're a violent man." He lifted his shoulders. "You frighten me. Sooner or later you'll be caught. You may not care for yourself, but there must be somebody in your life to care about."

"I'll ask you one more time," I answered. "What's Straight *got* on you? Why are you ready to see me crucified?"

He put his head in his hands. "All I can say is that I'm sorry for you."

The words rang in my brain. Lies, lies and lies. The truth was in the briefcase outside, the phone call he'd made from his office. But he knew the law better than I did. What evidence *was* there? Straight's past history could only arouse sympathy. And a quarter of a million pounds said he was sane. He'd set the board, manipulating me like a pawn in a game he meant to win.

"On your feet," I said.

I took him upstairs, waiting outside the bathroom door. Back in the bedroom, I made him strip to his underclothes and tied him up again. I left his mouth free. I undressed, blew the candle out, and crawled between the damp sheets. All the windows in the house were shut but I could hear the stutter of a motorcycle, the noise of a jet whining down to London airport. I was still awake when my ear caught the sound of a gate being opened. Pardoe was breathing heavily. I slipped out quietly into the hall and stood behind the curtain. A chink of light offered a head-on view of the driveway. A patrol car was drawn up twenty yards away. I watched a cop walk slowly toward the house. The window flared in the beam of his flashlight. It traveled the length of the lower floor, shifted above and then swept the garden. He turned on his heel and walked back to the prowl car. I heard him say something to the man at the wheel. Then the gate banged.

My watch was by the side of the bed. It was a few minutes past midnight. Almost certainly the house had been reported unoccupied. The visit was no more than a routine check. I crawled back into bed. Pardoe hadn't moved. For all I knew he was sleeping. I looked at him with dull hatred, thinking of Kirstie huddled alone and afraid.

135

Saturday

I DOZED through the long hours till daylight. Half past six. I went up and shaved. I found a clean shirt in a drawer in the closet. Something else caught my eye, a portable typewriter case. Early light filtered through the kitchen curtains. I boiled a couple of eggs, made tea and toast. When I finished breakfast I went into the bedroom. The courtroom image was gone. Pardoe's cheeks were covered with gray stubble. His eyes were bagged. I released him and he sat up, massaging his wrists and ankles. He started pulling his trousers on. I stopped him.

"You won't need those."

I took him up to the bathroom again and shoved the door open. "You've got five minutes." I heard him running water in the basin. He came out moving stiffly. He went down in front of me, hanging onto the banister rail. I jerked my head at the food on the table.

"Eat if you want."

He limped over and sat down. I straddled a chair in front of him. He still retained a sort of presence, even unshaven and in his underwear. His head was poised confidently as if time was his ally. He chewed through a piece of toast, drank two cups of tea, and asked me for a cigarette. I threw one on the table, added a box of matches.

He closed his eyes on the first long drag. He opened them again, considering the end of his cigarette.

"There's something you ought to know, Bain. A barrister is coming to my office at half past eleven this morning. If I'm not there, my secretary will phone my wife. She'll say that I've been called out of town. That's where your trouble starts."

"I'll live through it," I said shortly.

He smiled. "It's possible. But my secretary is a highly intelligent girl. She might well think that I have good reason for lying to my wife. But she'd never believe that I'd leave a senior member of the bar cooling his heels in my office without letting her know in advance. Without even picking the phone up and excusing myself to him."

His eyes betrayed him again. He was as desperate as I was behind the façade of equanimity. I crossed my arms on the back of the chair and lowered my chin onto them.

"I get it. If you could only speak to her, she'd be satisfied. There'd be no worried phone calls to the police. No hue and cry for Edward Pardoe."

He put his butt in his tea cup. "Strange as it sounds, I *don't* want the police looking for me. Because where I am, it seems that you'll be. And I don't want you caught. I've lied to you, Bain. I've tried to justify myself but it's no good. The truth is that it's Straight who's a sick man. There are things you don't know, things about his past history. I wouldn't have let you suffer. I wanted time to know what to do. Now my duty's clear."

"Bravo," I said softly. "And what does your conscience tell you?"

"To go to John with you," he answered steadily. "Persuade him to surrender. I know that together we can do it."

The chain of reasoning started with his secretary's suspicion and finished with a confrontation. One link was missing. I lifted my chin from my arm.

"Why us? Why not the police?"

He let his breath go. "I've known him twenty years. I wanted to spare him that. I can still think of him with compassion in spite of this dreadful thing. You see, I know the tragedy of his background. But I realize I can't expect a man in your position to feel as I do. You're right. You'd better call the police."

In one short speech he'd taken care of everything — acceptance of my innocence, the chance that I'd found his briefcase and read its contents. The last throwaway line was a masterpiece, delivered with dignified despair. He'd piled bluff on bluff with just one end in view. To put me safely in the hands of the law.

We looked at one another for fully a minute. His face already told me that he knew he'd lost. I stepped over the chair bringing the gun very close to his forehead. My hand was shaking.

"I never thought I'd want to use one of these things on a human being. But I'd put a bullet in your skull without a second's regret. *Up!*"

He played out the role, passing his hand wearily over his eyes and dragging his legs into the bedroom. I stuck the gag back in his mouth and tied him that much tighter. I left him rolled in a cocoon of sheets and blankets.

138

There was a sheaf of his headed notepaper in the briefcase. I took a piece of it to the dressing room with me and fed it into the typewriter. I addressed the letter to the Superintendent, Bramwell Grange Remedial Home, Olmer, Surrey.

Dear Sir,

This will introduce Mr. Marlow who is acting on behalf of the administrators of the John de Gruchy Straight Trust. Please facilitate any inquiries Mr. Marlow may wish to make concerning Mr. Straight's treatment while under your care.

This letter will constitute your authority to answer such questions as are compatible with professional etiquette.

Yours faithfully,
Edward Pardoe

I copied the signature on the Deed of Trust as best I could. I sealed the letter in an envelope and put it in my pocket. There were road maps and an atlas on the bookshelf. Olmer was a small dot between Woking and Leatherhead. I went down and opened the kitchen door. A leaden sky pressed outside, ominous and threatening. Bird tracks arrowed the frosted grass. I made my way to the road, keeping to the shelter of the beeches. The milk wagon thirty yards away was going in the opposite direction. I ran back to the garage and moved the Jaguar out.

Once released on the highway, the big car made time. Most of the traffic was headed the other way, aimed at the city. It was not yet ten when I turned off the highway. Olmer was posted as seven miles away. A mesh of lanes wormed between high banks, solid white lines a reminder of their narrowness. A mile outside the village was a sign: BRAMWELL GRANGE REMEDIAL HOME TWO HUNDRED YARDS LEFT.

139

A series of tight bends led to wrought iron gates set in weathered walls. Beyond the gates a plumb line of driveway ran to a Jacobean mansion a quarter of a mile distant. Dormer windows dotted the sharply slanted roofs. A woman in a head scarf appeared at the lodge door.

I lowered the window. "Where would I find the Superintendent?"

She came out a little further. "There's no superintendent here. Is it Doctor Posner you mean?"

I brandished the letter at her. "Will you tell him that someone from Mr. Pardoe's office would like to talk to him?"

She shifted to get a better look at me. "What name?"

"Pardoe," I called. "He'll know."

She disappeared inside. A post and rail fence lined the driveway. An old bay mare with a dropped belly was nuzzling the frosted grass. A hundred yards away, swans sailed on a reed-fringed lake. It was a few minutes before the woman emerged. The gates shuddered open.

"Miss Holly said to go up to the house. She'll be waiting for you."

The red hardtop took the noise out of the trees. The parkland merged into formal terraced gardens surrounding the rambling mansion. The driveway divided, the left fork curving round the back of the mansion, the right leading to broad stone steps. A white station wagon was parked in front of them. Painted on the side was the legend BRAMWELL GRANGE. I drew the Jaguar alongside. There were three crates of jigsaw puzzles in the back of the station wagon, a pile of paperbacks. The massive nail-studded door was open. A dark-haired girl in a long woolen dress and spectacles came forward smiling.

140

"Good morning. I'm Doctor Posner's secretary. I understand you've come from the solicitors?"

I raised my hat. "That's right. I have a letter for him. My name is Marlow."

"Will you come this way, please?" She led me across an enormous stone-flagged hall. The only furniture was a single bench against the wall. Two staircases curved up symmetrically. Someone upstairs was practicing scales on a trumpet. The noise stopped suddenly and a head hung through the banisters. Miss Holly ignored it, showing me into a room along a corridor.

"Wait here," she said brightly. "Doctor Posner's almost finished his rounds. He'll see you in a minute."

There were gay rugs on the polished floor, a bowl of bulbs on the table. Propped against a music stand was a card bearing Blake's *Auguries of Innocence*.

> To see the world in a grain of sand,
> And a heaven in a wild flower;
> Hold infinity in the palm of your hand,
> And eternity in an hour.

Oriel windows overlooked a classic maze of blackthorn. Beyond it, four men in track suits were playing a dispirited game of volleyball. I watched them for a while then the door opened. A tall stooped man came in wearing a surgical smock. He must have been in his late forties with cropped white hair and a sensitive face. He glanced at me over the tops of half-spectacles.

"Mr. Marlow?"

I gave him the letter. "I apologize for not phoning first, Doctor. I was pushed for time."

He smiled vaguely and tore the envelope with a fingernail. He read the letter through twice, lips forming the words.

"So," he said thoughtfully. "Will you please come with me?" His English was grammatical but strongly accented. He undid the door to the adjoining room. Floors and walls were aseptic, every corner rounded. There were more prints, some wild-looking paintings obviously done by patients. Hanging in the window was a cage with two budgerigars. Posner snapped his fingers, making chirruping sounds through pursed lips. He smiled as the birds locked bills.

"Such tenderness. Delightful, don't you think?"

His expression was innocently serious. He pushed a chair at me. He sat down behind the desk, joining long bony fingers.

"What is it you would like to know about John, Mr. Marlow?"

"I believe that two psychiatrists certified him sane. Were the examinations independent or was there just one?"

He frowned. "This I cannot tell you. Mr. Pardoe knows. We only heard about it from him by accident. John had been gone from our care for some time then." His eyes strayed toward the window. One of the birds was nibbling at its reflection in a tiny mirror.

"You'll have to excuse me," I explained. "But Mr. Pardoe's out of town. I haven't had the chance to see him yet."

His eyes were suddenly troubled. "I find this distressing, Mr. Marlow. Is something wrong? Has anything happened to John?"

142

I smiled to take the sting out of the words. "Please let me ask the questions, Doctor Posner. And I'd be grateful for a frank answer. Is there any record of violence in John Straight's history here?"

"*Wiolence!*" Indignation stopped him from finding the right consonant. He got up, his sweeping hand taking in the scene through the windows. "What do you see there — beauty or ugliness, Mr. Marlow? Flowers, plants, creepers — many of them unknown outside Kew Gardens! All of it was John's work. This was his *home*. He was here many years, even before I came. I must tell you that restraint here is minimal. There is no need. Our patients are chosen carefully. No, sir. When John left us, violence would have been beyond his understanding."

There was no doubt of his sincerity. The next question I put bluntly.

"You say this was his home. Who took him away, Pardoe or his family?"

He took a turn to the birdcage and back, head bent and hands clasped. He spoke with obvious feeling.

"John *had* no family, except one brother. In former times this was a very real relationship. Gradually it weakened. The last time John saw his brother must have been five years ago. To someone in my position, the pattern is all too familiar. The more fortunate are disturbed by mental sickness. There is a tendency to rationalize by avoidance. John is a sensitive being. His brother's indifference wounded him deeply. But he never spoke of it. He had difficulty in communicating. What he did was retreat deeper and deeper into his own world. The world of plants and flowers. These he knew would never fail him."

143

The discrepancy between the man he described and the one I knew baffled me. It seemed incredible that a few short months could have changed a simple-minded gardener into a calculating killer. I tried another tack.

"You spoke about mental sickness, Doctor. Just how far gone *was* John?"

He worried an earlobe. "How shall I answer you? This is a question of different areas. He knew the difference between right and wrong, certainly. We were surprised here to learn of his complete recovery, so quickly. It seemed contrary to reason, to years of clinical observation. Of course I have no knowledge of the tests applied. Often the human brain works its own miracles. A deeply traumatic experience can unbalance a sane mind. Equally so, the same degree of shock can give an appearance of sanity to a disordered mind. You see what I say, Mr. Marlow: 'An appearance of sanity.' The unhappy fact is that too often this is only temporary. This is what worries me when you talk of John."

This made more sense. Suppose the news of Mark's suicide had shocked John into temporary sanity. He could have reverted, his condition aggravated by the death of a brother he worshiped. The next crazy step would be to kill the woman he held responsible.

I lit a fresh butt. "When was John first certified insane?"

He looked at me blankly. "He was never certified! From a legal point of view, he was a voluntary patient. Quite obviously we would not have allowed him to leave without taking the necessary precautions for his safety."

"But he *did* leave," I reminded him.

He made a defensive gesture. "I am trying to explain. John

was a voluntary patient. He was discharged to the care of his trustees. He left the institution with Mr. Pardoe and a male nurse we recommended. The board here had no option. I realize you are only carrying out your instructions but I must insist on knowing the reasons for these questions."

I had to calm him down. It wasn't the moment to start him on a witch-hunt of his own.

"I'm sorry," I said. "I seem to have made things sound a whole lot worse than they really are. The fact is that John's behavior has been giving anxiety to the trustees. He's shown signs of violence, irresponsibility with money. And there are large sums at stake. There's a difference of opinion among the trustees. The bank would like him retested. It's a difficult situation."

Posner exploded, his eyes angry above his spectacles. "Banks! Money! This is no matter for laymen. You are dealing with the human brain, Mr. Marlow!"

I hurried reassurance. "That's the real purpose of my visit, Doctor, to get your reaction. I can promise you that all Mr. Pardoe wants is John's complete recovery. You spoke of a male nurse. Could you let me have his address?"

He looked at me narrowly. "You're putting John back in Redfern's care?"

The lead was a lucky one. "That's the general idea."

His face showed relief. "That makes me happy. He could not be in better hands." He scribbled an address on a piece of paper and gave it to me.

I tucked the briefcase under my arm and rose. "You've been very helpful, Doctor. My apologies for taking up so much of your time."

145

He opened the door. "Not at all. This may sound strange to you, Mr. Marlow but we are a close community here. Everyone was sad to see John go. We were all very fond of him. I should be glad if you would let me know what happens."

"Somebody will," I said. He came to the top of the steps with me. He waved as I drove off. The woman at the lodge had the gates open, ready for me. Round the first bend, I stopped the car and read the piece of paper Posner had given me. George Redfern, 22 Blackshaw Road, Chiswick.

There was still time to make it there before meeting Kirstie. I put the car in gear. The powerful motor responded, eating up the miles once I hit the highway. The radio was beamed to Channel Two. An announcer's voice cut in with a news flash. Miss World faints after investiture; more pressure on the pound; fresh outbreaks of foot-and-mouth disease. No mention of a man wanted to help in a murder investigation. I switched the set off. The police network would be less reticent. Foster would have dug back in my file by now, checking all known associates, the people I'd done time with, the places I'd worked. My world was shrinking by the hour.

I turned west on Chiswick Road, pulling up at a pub on the corner. A couple of troubled thinkers were waiting for the doors to open.

I called over to one of them. "Blackshaw Road?"

He answered without detaching himself from the wall. "Second on your left, past the school."

I drove down a short street facing the river. The small houses stood in pairs in the sad suburban morning, each a replica of its neighbor. Three rooms up, two down. The street doors were side by side, separated only by a low fence.

A blind man could have tapped his way into any one of them and felt at home. There'd be the same smell of boiled cabbage, the same monotonous beat from the radio.

Twenty-two was the last house on the right. A shingle on the gate read *George Redfern M.R.N.*

I put the tinted glasses away in my pocket. A motor scooter was propped in the front yard, a bundle of fishing rods strapped along the framework. Crisscrossed nylon curtains moved as I made my way up the path. I didn't have a chance to use the doorbell.

A man appeared, wearing carpet slippers and a thick turtleneck sweater. He blocked the doorway with stocky arms, eyes snapping in a crumpled face. A half-inch of gray stubble covered his scalp as if it had just been planted there. He looked at the briefcase under my arm.

"Don't want anything," he said shortly.

I shifted my legs. "Mr. Redfern? Doctor Posner gave me your address."

He hung onto the door, shaking his head. "No cases. I'm on holiday."

"I won't be long," I urged. "It's about an ex-patient of yours, Mr. John Straight."

A second inspection of me left him unmoved. "What about him?"

"Couldn't we talk inside?" I suggested. "I'll be as brief as I can."

His manner was short of gracious but he let me into the house. He opened a door. It might well have been a showroom in any neighborhood furniture store. A stained table and matching chairs. A heavily beveled mirror hanging on a gilt chain. Mock logs in a glazed-tile fireplace. I groped in my pocket, feeling automatically for my cigarettes. He lifted a restraining hand.

"No smoking in here, if you don't mind. Is it Pardoe who sent you?"

The way he said it warned me to hedge. "I'm employed by Mr. Straight's trustees. I'll be frank with you. He's had a relapse and they're worried. You probably know, there are large sums involved."

"Worried, are they?" He settled down comfortably on his chair. The room was like a refrigerated boxcar but he seemed totally unaware of it. "What are you then, a lawyer?"

"I'm an inquiry agent," I answered patiently. "And I'm trying to get an over-all picture of Straight's treatment after he left Bramwell. Don't ask me why. There are a lot of inquiry agents around. I just do as I'm told."

He inserted his hand into the neck of his sweater and eased it.

"What you say your name was?"

"Marlow," I answered.

He leaned forward, stabbing a bunch of frankfurter-fingers at me.

"Well you listen to me, Mr. Marlow. I've been a nurse for twenty-four years, half of them in the Navy. You could say that I've had patients from all walks of life. There's drawers full of letters upstairs, people I've helped. I don't *have* to go out with a drum and beat up patients. And I never had one whipped away from me without as much as a thank you. Not till I met your Mister-bloody-Pardoe."

"I see what you mean," I agreed. "I'm glad you're talking

like this. It'll interest the trustees, I mean, the others. All they know is what Pardoe told them."

He blew his nose hard. "If ever a poor bugger needed friends it was him. Not a load of bankers sitting round a table counting his money."

I waited till I was sure of his attention. "I ought to tell you, Mr. Redfern, there's no suggestion that your treatment wasn't satisfactory. Straight left Bramwell in your care in March, right? What happened then?"

"What *happened?*" He ticked the points off on stubby fingers. "We went down to this vicarage — Aldbourne, it was, in Sussex. Pardoe said he'd taken it for a year. John and I were supposed to stay there the summer at least. We were alone. He was no trouble. It was like living with an overgrown schoolboy. He messed about outside, putting bulbs in the garden and the like. I even taught him how to use a rod. Poor sod."

I roped him back to the main issue. "Did you stay there all summer?"

He dropped his hands, staring at me as if I'd said his slip was showing.

"You must be joking! We were there ten days exactly! Then Pardoe arrived. 'Pack John's things. He's leaving immediately.' No explanations, no thanks, nothing. Oh, I got my check, yes. It's as well for him that I did," he added darkly.

It was almost noon and my feet were freezing. "Didn't Pardoe say that he was taking John to the Hayley Memorial Clinic?"

"He didn't say *nothing!*" Redfern reiterated. "Look, I'm

an ex-serviceman. I've dealt with some rough buggers in my day, admirals who'd bite your ear off for the wrong kind of look. But I never run up against a pig like that Pardoe. It's men like him make people vote Communist."

He made it sound the ultimate in criticism. I got the last question in quickly.

"Did Posner tell you that John was examined by psychiatrists in August, that they declared him sane?"

His voice was heavy with emphasis. "I haven't seen nor heard from Posner since March. I've been away on a case. But if what you say's true, it's the psychiatrists who need their heads examined."

He sat back, his crumpled face stubborn. The interview was obviously at an end.

"Thanks for your help," I said. "You'll be hearing from us, Mr. Redfern."

He came as far as the hall with me. "I don't *want* to hear from you. I'm going to be down on the Test River, tickling trout, for the next three weeks. But watch that Pardoe. Take it from me. He's no good, mate."

The door was closed firmly. I crossed the street, restraining the impulse to look back. The sky seemed to have dropped even lower. It was cold with the acrid threat of fog. I turned the car round and headed east, windows up and the heater going full blast. I wheeled the heavy machine automatically, making all the right moves with the exaggeration of a man taking a driving test.

It's hard to describe how I felt. Everything seemed to be done within a framework of fear, a chronic condition that my brain had accepted. Doubt whittled away at each new hope.

The sixty-four-dollar question came up repeatedly. Was this the sort of love Kirstie deserved — a blank check demand on her loyalty? Yet in spite of everything, justice was as important as love. And I wasn't thinking of a female in a Grecian robe and a blindfold. My justice was the avenger with an axe, waiting for the signal to let it fall. My signal.

I cut through St. John's Wood and down Prince Albert Road. I took one of the tiny bridges over the canal onto the Outer Circle. Near the main zoo entrance I slackened speed. A frantic-looking man in a dufflecoat was jockeying a crowd of short-trousered hooligans through the turnstiles. Camera-hung tourists clustered round the peanut vendors. It was five to one and no Kirstie. I drove on, looking for a place to leave the car. An unbroken line of vehicles crowded the curb ahead. I took the next bridge back onto Prince Albert Road. This was even worse, no waiting or unloading.

Ornate blocks of flats lined the north side of the road, their opulent fronts facing the green sweep of Regent's Park. The near-deserted forecourts were tempting. I remembered the card stuck under the windshield wiper. But lightning didn't strike the same place twice and this wasn't embassy property. I pulled into the nearest entrance.

A low brick wall separated the concourse from the sidewalk. I killed the motor, looking over at the plate glass doors at the top of the steps. A porter was talking to the mink-wrapped matron just inside the lobby. I slipped out of the car, locking up on the blind side. I was halfway to the street when I heard the shouting behind me. The porter fetched up, hatless and blowing. He aimed the words with the aggressiveness of the small man in uniform, arm thrown out at the sign near the wall.

151

"Can't you read — Private Property! This is for residents only."

I fished a couple of coins out of my pocket. "You didn't see me."

The woman in the lobby was peering through the glass doors. He positioned himself dramatically.

"I saw you right enough. And I'm telling you to move that car!"

It was a simple enough proposition. It was the mean face soaked in petty authority that did something to me.

"I'll move it. But you'd better get back in your kennel. I wouldn't want to cause an accident."

The next few seconds ground out in slow motion. I saw the flat cap of a cop on the sidewalk, the porter's expression of triumph. He bawled over the wall.

"D'y'mind coming over here, Officer. I'm having a bit of trouble."

He planted himself squarely in front of me, scowling like Edward G. Robinson. The cop vaulted over the wall. He was young but he'd obviously learned fast. He'd mastered the slow stroll, the thumb hooked strategically near the whistle. The porter got in first.

"This man doesn't live here, Officer. I asked him to move his car and he threatened me."

The cop looked me up and down. "No threat," I said. "All I did was tell him to get out of the way."

The cop glanced across at the Jaguar. "Better move it, sir, if you've no business on the premises."

I walked over and unlocked the car. I thought that he'd gone but he was waiting outside the entrance. He held his hand up and I stopped. He came round to my window, pulling his notebook out. He copied the particulars from the tax sticker on the windshield.

"Is this your car, sir?"

I seemed to have done it all before in a nightmare ending in disaster.

"It's my car, yes." I reached for the papers in the glove compartment.

His eyes missed nothing, taking in the briefcase on the seat beside me. "Got your driving license and insurance with you?"

Shaking fingers found the small red folder and certificate. He inspected both documents thoroughly before returning them to me. The bag with the gun and skeleton keys was underneath my seat. I had a job keeping my voice normal.

"I don't get it, Officer. What am I supposed to have done?"

He snapped the elastic on his notebook, the star pupil when the rest of the class is lost.

"Take a look at your front number plate, sir. I couldn't read it with my nose on the radiator. The law says twenty yards."

He walked off, leaving me staring at the ticket in my lap. I tucked it between the pages of the driving license. The cop sauntered away slowly to the strains of an unheard march. I felt I'd just been ejected from a spin dryer. It might be months before the summons was processed. But I suddenly wanted no more part of the Jaguar. I put the bag with the gun and keys in the briefcase and made a quick U-turn. I drove into a garage at the bottom of Primrose Hill and asked for a suspension check. The works manager listened attentively to a fictitious account of noises on bends. Sounded like shock absorbers, he said. But it might be steering trouble. He'd have to get the car up on the hoist. If I wanted to leave it, he'd have a report for me by Tuesday. I signed an authority for the work to be done and got out as fast as I could.

Twenty past one. The strangled roar of the lions reached me long before I came to the zoo entrance. My eye caught the bright emerald green of Kirstie's coat. She was standing near the ticket office. The only man near her was a man holding a string of balloons. I passed the line of parked cars, looking straight ahead, ready to break at the first sign of danger. Kirstie saw me as I crossed the road. She came two steps to meet me. I shook my head, hurrying past her through the turnstiles. Twenty yards on I stopped and looked back. She'd already bought her ticket and was following. I walked on in the direction of the elephant house, the feral smell of the big cats rank in my nose. The schoolboys I'd seen earlier were whooping in front of the cages. The duffle-coated man in charge of them seemed to have given up, contenting himself with an occasional bawl as one of them neared disaster.

Kirstie pushed her way through the shouting group. Her cheek was cold against my mouth. I held her arm tight as we sat down on the bench. Her whole body was shaking. She opened her handbag, took a newspaper out and gave it to me. Her eyes were close to tears. The paper was folded at an inside page. The report seemed to take on three dimensions.

WIDOW'S DEATH SPARKS HUNT FOR MAN

From our crime correspondent
Leaflets giving the description of a Canadian were being distributed today throughout the Metropolitan Police area. Mrs. Jessica

154

Straight, 36, was found dead yesterday morning in her Kingston Hill luxury home. Police believe that the Canadian, Macbeth Bain, aged 36 with an address in Fulham, can assist their enquiries. Bain is of medium-build, height 5'11" with brown graying hair and blue eyes. He may be wearing a sports-jacket, fawn corduroy trousers, and brown rubber-soled shoes. Police visited addresses in the West End, late last night in an attempt to interview Bain. A watch on the ports and air terminals is being maintained.

There was a refuse bin behind the bench. I tossed the newspaper into it, feeling as though I'd been sandbagged. At the back of my mind had always been a faint hope that if it came to it, I could still give myself up. That there'd still be an area of doubt a man like Foster would move into incisively. I knew now that I was right and Kirstie was wrong. This meant that every chance of help was cut off. Police informers all over town would be sniffing the breeze expectantly. The world beyond the law treated murder like a contagious disease, contaminating whoever it touched. People like Riffkind and Hickey would block their brains against my memory, already weighing the possibilities of being questioned.

Kirstie clung to my hand. "It was on the news this morning. Daddy telephoned at half past seven."

A man and woman passed in front of us. He dropped an empty peanut bag in the refuse bin, laughing as he turned to his companion. I stared at their backs stonily.

"That must have been interesting. Even in his wildest moments he couldn't have hoped for better. Not only a thief but a murderer."

She pulled away, looking at me as if I'd struck her across the face.

"What are you trying to do to me? I can't stand it. He's

155

my *father*. Don't you realize what he's going through? He wants me to go down there. He even threatened to come and fetch me."

I lifted a shoulder. "Then go." At least there'd be no more doubt, no more soul-searching. "I mean it," I affirmed.

She blinked hard. "And what would happen to you?"

The question was for herself but I answered it. "I'll still have something going for me. I know all there is about running, about being alone. It'll soon be over anyway."

Her tears spilled over. "What does that mean?"

It seemed that bitterness had become part of my voice. "I'll lay it on the nose, take a good look at me. There isn't one mother's son who's read that report who wouldn't jump me given the chance. It's my life they all want, no less. I love you, Kirstie, but I know what I've got to do."

She was still struggling to keep her mouth under control. She peeled her glove off and imprisoned my hand in the warmth of her fingers.

"Don't ever *say* you're alone. I wanted you to give yourself up but that was yesterday. All that matters now is to be with you, for as long as you need me, darling."

A perverse will to lose drove me on. "If they find us together they'll drag you into it. Your friend Foster won't be choosy. You could even be charged as an accessory after the act."

Her small face flared with anger. "I don't care *what* they do to me! Do you suppose I slept last night? All I could do was lie there and worry about you. I know you didn't kill that woman. That's what matters."

My heart slipped back into place. "Then I'll promise you this. It's facts now not guesswork. I've seen the doctor in charge at Bramwell. Pardoe took Straight away with a male nurse. I've talked with him too. They were going to spend the whole summer at some house in Sussex. But the nurse only had him for a few days. Then Pardoe showed up. He paid off the nurse and took Straight away again, to the clinic this time. And in seventeen weeks they're supposed to have done what the other place couldn't do in as many years. The doctor at Bramwell doesn't believe it. The nurse doesn't believe it. I don't believe it."

She stared at the cigarette between her gloved fingers as though wondering how it got there. She leaned forward, one hand holding the curve of hair away from the match.

"I did what you told me to do, telephoned my doctor. The psychiatrists who signed that certificate are two of the top men in the country."

The news didn't worry me too much. I told her why. "I don't care *who* they are, not anymore. Posner's been treating these cases for years. He says shock can make a sick brain sane. But the chances are that it won't last. Maybe these two psychiatrists knew nothing about Straight's past history — or no more than Pardoe wanted them to know. All they were asked to say was that at a given time and place Straight passed whatever tests they made on him. Maybe he did. What does it prove. They might have only seen him for a couple of hours. What about the Hayley Memorial?"

She shook her head. "He'd never heard of it. I called the Ministry of Health this morning. All they'll say is that it's a privately-run clinic specializing in remedial surgery."

Remedial home, remedial surgery. A signal kept flashing in my mind, a subconscious memory demanding recognition. And then I had it.

157

"Wait a minute, Kirstie. There's an operation they do on these people — prefrontal lobotomy. That would account for the size of the bill."

"I don't know," she said uncertainly. Something was troubling her. Her eyes wavered. "I've got to tell you this, darling," she went on. "*I'm* almost sure that no one followed me to the hairdresser's. But there was a man standing on the corner last night. I saw him as I got out of the taxi. He was there again this morning when I went to work, just by the post office."

"Are you certain?" I asked sharply. They traveled in pairs. She might have missed his companion. "What did he look like?"

She ground her heel on her cigarette, thinking. "About your height, a dark hat and coat. I couldn't see him too well last night and this morning I didn't want to look. But I know it was the same man."

It was no time to disturb her with the incident about the Jaguar.

"You could be mistaken. OK, we'll play it doubly safe. The clinic's where the answers are. Did you bring any money with you?"

She pulled an envelope out of her handbag. "I told the bank to cash some War Bonds. There's fifty pounds there, I've kept seventy."

Her eyes followed the movement of my hand as I undid the briefcase. She must have sensed that the gun was inside.

"*Please,*" she said impulsively. "Give it to me. I'll throw it in the water somewhere."

"There's no need," I lied. "It's empty."

She smoothed the thin skin gloves over her fingers nervously. "Aren't you going to listen to me at all, not even about Pardoe?"

I looked at her blankly. *"Pardoe?"*

Hazel eyes pleaded with me. "Can't you let him go? I've got a feeling something terrible's going to happen. He frightens me."

"Then the line forms on the right," I answered. "He frightens me too. But next to him I'm a beginner. That's why he's staying where he is. One thing is sure, Kirstie. We've got him going. He knows it's a matter of time. I can tell it." I signaled her to her feet. The class of animal lovers was coming down the path toward us, bombing one another with paper sacks full of water. I steered her away hurriedly.

"What did you do about your father?"

She walked very close to me, imprisoning my arm. "I phoned him last night. I thought the police would be listening. I said I hadn't seen you for days, that I'd be coming down at the weekend."

She took my silence for disapproval. "You don't think I'm going, do you? I'll invent some excuse. I just had to put his mind at rest."

"I'm thinking of something else," I replied. "What's happening at the office?"

Caged birds on our right were raucous. I could scarcely hear her answer.

"Brice called me in as soon as I got there this morning. He told me to go home. It was just as well, I wasn't making sense. My secretary knows. She'd read the papers and remembered your name. I'm not sure about the others."

159

"The hell with the others," I burst out. "It's Foster I'm concerned with. We've got to be dead certain you're not followed when we meet. Do you think you can do it?"

We covered twenty yards before she spoke. "I've got to. I was thinking about it all night. I've found a way to get in and out of the block without being seen. Does that help?"

I glanced down at her, doubting that I'd heard correctly. "You're damned right it helps, provided you don't act suspiciously. How?"

I slowed up for her. She was taking two steps to my one. "Over the roof," she said. "There's a fire escape down to that yard where the porter keeps his ladders and things. The door's always locked because of the kids. You know where it is, round the corner. Nobody'd see me go out."

I pulled her to a halt, swinging her round to face me. "That wall's twelve feet high. How do you propose getting over it?"

She lifted her handbag. "I've already got the key to the door."

I couldn't help smiling. "You missed your vocation, you're a burglar at heart. Now listen — the only time you can use that door is after nightfall. You can't walk about on the roof in broad daylight, understand? Where's your car?"

"In the garage," she said. "I put it in for servicing. I thought it would look better. As long as I was using it, they'd know where I was."

I shook my head at her. "Now I'm certain you're a rogue. Then here's what you do. Go straight out to one of the big car rental firms. Choose something fast but inconspicuous. You know the steps leading down to the Mall from Carlton

House Terrace? I'll be waiting at the bottom at six-fifteen. OK?"

She might have been afraid but she wasn't showing it. "OK."

I watched her leave, feeling that every time I kissed her might be the last. I gave it ten minutes then followed her out. I walked up into Camden Town and had something to eat in a hamburger joint. I moved next door into a movie theater. For the next couple of hours I watched the screen with a sense of unreality. Problems were resolved to a crescendo of sound from an unseen string orchestra. The wrap-up message was inspiring. Good triumphed over evil.

It was past four when I left the theater and flagged down a cab. The driver wanted double money to take me out to Hampton Court. He started to give me the bit about not finding a fare to bring him back. I cut him short and climbed in, sitting in the corner with my eyes shut. Kirstie was right. Pardoe was an encumbrance, an old-man-of-the-sea I'd saddled myself with. But the only place I could dump him was in Foster's lap. Meanwhile he was a prisoner to be guarded and fed. Every time I went back to the house I ran the risk of being seen. A chance observer walking a dog or mailing a letter. Someone who'd know that I had no right there.

It was a long time afterwards when I looked out of the window. I recognized the arched span of lights and tapped on the glass partition.

"This'll do. You can let me off here."

He pulled over to the curb at the foot of the rise. He stuffed the money I gave him into a tobacco pouch, looking up the mist-banked river.

"Eleven more bleeding hours of," he observed feelingly. "Gawd knows why I do it."

I opened the cab door. "If you think of the answer let me know."

Street lamps were already lit along the deserted road. I could see more lights through the meshed branches, a hundred yards or so away. I slipped through the gate and waited. I heard nothing. A late-feeding bird rose underfoot as I crossed the lawn to the back door. It whirred away into the beech trees with a shrill call of alarm. The house looked as if it were etched against the sky. The refrigerator motor clicked on as I opened the door. I put the briefcase in a cupboard under the sink and turned the handle of the bedroom door. I shone the flash on Pardoe's face. His eyes were open. I untied him, gesturing with the gun.

"If you want the john, move."

He shambled off the bed in socks and underwear, favoring his right leg. I suspected the business with the leg and kept close to him all the way upstairs. The cistern was flushed. He came out, pushing his hand through his hair, watching me furtively. I lit the candle in the kitchen, sliced the top off a can of corned beef and made him a rough sandwich. He was just about to put his teeth into it when the phone rang.

"Stay where you are," I warned.

We faced one another, suspended in time, waiting for an unseen hand to lift the receiver. The bell stopped ringing as unexpectedly as it had started. His tongue licked over his lips and I knew what he was thinking.

"Sorry, wrong number," I said.

He didn't answer. I gave him a glass of water. He drank it slowly. I motioned him to his feet. He lay face down on his bed as I roped his wrists back to his ankles. He turned over, widening his mouth for the gag. Our eyes met. His were stony with hate. I knotted the sheet even tighter and chucked a blanket over him. The air in the room was exhausted. I left the bedroom door ajar and went upstairs again.

The newspaper Kirstie had brought had lit a fresh fuse under me. The description given of my clothing was no longer accurate. And Hickey at least knew it. At a time like this, relying on the Old Pal's Act was a quick way of committing suicide. I couldn't take the chance he wouldn't step into some phone booth, an anonymous voice supply an up-to-date report of the clothes I was wearing. I pulled a tweed coat from a hanger in the dressing room. It was a fair fit. I left the tinted glasses in the pocket of my mac.

The briefcase had become part of my uniform. I pulled it out of the cupboard and locked the back door behind me. It was almost dark outside, the mist ghostly over the water. I pushed through dripping trees to the boundary wall. The street was still empty. I climbed over, dropping down on the sidewalk and walking off briskly.

Street lamps became more frequent, suburban villas replacing the isolated splendor of the houses behind me. Children's voices greeted the return of the homing breadwinners. Doors slammed. Dogs barked. Drawn curtains shut out the murky cold. There wasn't a hope of finding a cab. It was ten minutes before the first bus appeared. I rode it as far as Richmond and switched to the subway. I surfaced at Trafalgar Square, buttoning up against the raw night. The stone lions were somber against the floodlit façade of the National Gallery. I crossed Cockspur Street a few minutes early for my rendezvous with Kirstie. Beyond Admiralty Arch a dark expanse of park stretched to the lighted turrets of Victoria Street. Somewhere among the new skyscrapers was Scotland Yard.

I positioned myself at the bottom of the steps. Traffic was filtering into the Mall, headlights flaring. Six-fifteen. Six-twenty. Suddenly a car pulled out of the mainstream, signaling a lefthand turn. It stopped twenty yards from me. I recognized the shape of Kirstie's head but stayed where I was, making sure nothing was following her. I ran across and opened the car door. We sat for a moment, locked desperately. "Don't let it stop," I begged. I knew that it was the same for her, that every time we parted was the last.

I let her go, checking the car. It was a brand new Ford, fast and inconspicuous. She trailed her hand over the seat, touching the back of my neck with it.

"What is it?" I asked quietly. "There's something bothering you."

"It's Daddy," she admitted. "I called him to say I couldn't go down. I told him I was spending the weekend with a girl friend. A reporter's been pestering them. The man's supposed to have been trying to reach me. He left a number . . ."

I screwed my head round. "Don't tell me you called it!"

Her face was miserable. "I had to do *something*. My mother was in tears. You know how they live. Nothing that happens in that village is secret. The man mentioned your name. He even suggested going down there."

The bastards would stop at nothing. "Did he tell you what newspaper he worked for?" I put in quickly.

"I didn't ask," she answered. "All I wanted was to make sure he didn't bother my parents anymore. He asked me if I'd be at home this evening. I told him the same story, that I was spending the weekend with friends. Then this shook me rigid — he asked if I had been in touch with Pardoe. I said I'd never even heard of him and the man laughed. Just as if he knew I was lying. Then he hung up."

I did my best to comfort her. "Bluff, darling. There are a dozen ways he could have gotten hold of Pardoe's name. But he'll be back. The next time he rings, if he shows up at the flat, threaten to call the cops."

She didn't sound convinced. "You didn't talk to him," she objected. "He was so *sure* of himself."

I moved my hand from side to side. "All he was sure of was your reaction. These creeps are after a story, the more sensational the better. 'Brigadier's daughter linked with murder suspect.' He's not going to want to miss that. Do you still have his number?"

She poked around in her handbag. "City 0964."

"Let me take care of it," I promised. "Move over."

We changed places. She wrapped her coat round her knees. "Where are we going?"

"To the clinic." I made a few dummy passes with the gearshift. "I've just caught on, we're going to take a leaf from their own book. You'll have to do the talking, darling. You're a reporter covering Jessica Straight's killing. Your angle is wholesale tragedy. Mark Straight's suicide and all the rest of it. Make it plain that you know about his brother's mental history. You want to know what happened to him at the clinic."

She was silent. I caught the worried expression on her face. "Won't they ask what newspaper I work for?"

I unfastened her handbag. A sheaf of calling cards was in a pocket of her wallet. I took one out.

> *Kirstie Kirkpatrick*
> *Universal Publicity Services*
> *Tufnell House,*
> *Fleet St. E.C.1.*

"Just show them one of these if they do. Say you've got a tie-up with an overseas agency. Either they'll talk or they won't."

I turned the car in a tight circle, waiting for a chance to ease into the westbound traffic.

"If we're stopped for any reason at all, leave the answers to me."

It took an hour to reach Sunningdale Village. I pulled up outside a freeway Tudor inn. The parking lot was empty. I left Kirstie in the car and went into the pub. A fire was burning in the bar. Horse brasses glittered on the walls. The one man in the room was sitting behind the beer handles. He looked up slowly from his newspaper.

"Could you direct me to the Hayley Memorial Clinic?" I asked.

His smile was ironical. "Something told me you weren't a customer. All I seem to do since they brought this bloody test out is sit here and act as an information bureau. Which way are you facing?"

I showed him. He ducked beneath a flap in the bar and came to the door with me.

"Keep going till you see a sign. GOLF COURSE, it says. Turn left. This'll bring you to the clubhouse. You turn right. You'll find the clinic half a mile up the road."

I got back behind the wheel. Five hundred yards on, a cut-off ran straight over the brow of a hill. It switch-backed for a mile or so then the headlamps picked out turf scarred with sand traps. There was a glimpse of a swimming pool in front of a timber-built clubhouse. I turned right. The road ran between the fairway and a dense stand of Sitka spruce. A sign glimmered. HAYLEY MEMORIAL CLINIC. NO HORNS PLEASE.

I stopped the Ford and killed the lights. I transferred the gun and keys to my overcoat under cover of the sudden darkness.

"Wait here," I said. "I want to look around."

She reached out to touch me. "Be careful."

The driveway was strung with wire. I climbed between the strands and walked into the spruce thicket. The glow ahead grew brighter as I progressed. Unexpectedly I had reached the edge of the plantation. Fifty yards away, a glass-and-steel structure soared above the tops of the trees. The clinic was T-shaped, the front of it the lateral bar. Most of the windows were lit. The building looked like the bridge of some ocean liner, high above a sea of spruce. More lights showed in a complex of annexes behind. A door opened nearby. I ducked low as a nurse in a cape came out. She passed near enough for me to hear her humming.

She went through the double glass doors into the white lobby. A box sign over a side entrance read ambulances. I watched her stop at the desk, talk to the nurse already sitting there. Then she disappeared. I made my way back to the car. Kirstie's cigarette was a point of red behind the windshield. I spoke through the window.

"It's all yours, darling. Don't let them brush you off. Be obstinate. Don't forget, you want the man in charge."

She nodded and switched on the motor. I climbed back through the fence and trotted after the retreating taillights. By the time I reached the clearing, she was already in the lobby talking to the nurse at the desk. I could see them both clearly, the nurse shaking her head, Kirstie fumbling in her handbag. Then they both went out of sight.

The hardtop concourse ran flush to the front wall. There were no bushes there — once I was out of the trees, no cover. Nothing but the stark wall, steel-framed windows marking what looked like administration offices. A mouse couldn't have made it unobserved.

Kirstie had left the Ford smack outside the front entrance. The longer she stayed in there, the better our chances. I worked my way back through the trees to the end of the wing. Most of the windows in the main block were curtained. A covered way connected it with a flat-roofed annex. My guess was a morgue. Music was coming from a dormitory building behind. I heard the sound of women's voices then the noise of a car being started. I raced back to my vantage point. The Ford was vanishing down the driveway. A man was talking to two nurses in the lobby.

I stumbled through the darkness, over the fence, and onto the road. All I could hear was the sound of my own breathing. The car was parked a hundred yards away. I ran on toward it.

Kirstie was lying over the steering wheel, head hidden between her arms. I disengaged them gently. She reached out
blindly for me, sobbing.

"They *telephoned* him!"

I wiped her eyes with my handkerchief. "Telephoned
who?" My handkerchief was a soggy ball already. She took
it from me, fighting the catch in her voice.

"Straight. I've let you down."

I lit a cigarette for her. The match flare showed her face
abject. The words tumbled out.

"There was this nurse. I told her I just had to speak to
someone in authority. She wouldn't even listen at first, then
I showed her the card. That seemed to impress her. She
spoke to someone on the phone. Dr. Leonard would see me,
she said." Her voice broke again. "I thought I was doing so
well."

I gripped her tightly by the shoulders. "What *happened,*
Kirstie?"

She lifted her head. "A doctor arrived. I told him exactly
what you said. The first thing he asked was what paper I
represented. I showed him the card as you said."

"For Crissakes, Kirstie," I argued. "I *know* what I said. I
want to know what *he* said."

Her voice was quieter. "He was horrible. Red-haired and
sly. He just sat there turning the card over in his fingers,
looking at me without saying anything. I thought he was just
making his mind up whether or not to give me a story. Suddenly he started attacking me, talking about intrusion into
personal grief. I must have looked completely stupid. I
couldn't think what to answer. Then he picked up the phone.
He said he was going to call Straight, that he'd answer any

169

question that Straight authorized. There *wasn't* anything I could do, Macbeth, only sit there stupidly, watching him dial."

I pitched the butt through the window. "It isn't your fault, honey. I should never have sent you in."

She gripped my hand hard and let it go. "The doctor read my name and address from the card. I could hear Straight's voice quite plainly. He sounded angry. 'These people are making my life a misery, Doctor,' he said. 'Thank you for letting me know. Just get rid of her.'"

I couldn't remember seeing her as defeated-looking as she was at that moment. We'd faced enough trouble together before. But she'd always defied it. She'd even insisted on speaking for me at my trial.

She'd stood in the witness box, answering counsel's questions with a courage and dignity that impressed the whole court. Even the judge had mentioned it. *The jury have found you guilty on overwhelming evidence, Bain. I can find nothing in your record that warrants the leniency counsel is asking for. Had it not been for Miss Kirkpatrick's belief in you, the sentence I propose to pass would have been considerably longer. You'll do well to remember that.*

I'd never forgotten. Yet without her courage my own was nothing.

"Listen to me," I begged. "For God's sake, try to understand what's happened. Why do you think Straight didn't tell the doctor to call the police? He *knows* who you really are, that they're hoping to find me through you. I'll tell you why, because the last thing he wants is police at the clinic."

I felt the nervous movement of her body. "He knows where I live."

170

I couldn't bring myself to tell her how much the thought was worrying me.

"He won't come anywhere near you, darling. The fact that you've been here's enough to put him on his guard, I'll give you that. He's desperate but he isn't a fool. You're the last person he'll approach. He can't even be sure you're not acting under police instructions." More than anything I wanted this last flimsy hope to be a possibility.

"That's right," she agreed. "He can't be sure, can he?" I knew she didn't believe it, that she was forcing herself to show the courage I needed.

"I've got to go back in there, Kirstie. Think carefully. Where did you see the doctor? Upstairs, downstairs? How far away was it from where the nurse sits?"

Her fingers curled in my palm as she pondered. "About twenty feet. The room's on the left of the lobby."

I visualized the front of the building. Some of the windows there had been in darkness.

"Can you remember seeing anything that looked like a filing cabinet, anywhere that records might be kept?"

She shook her head. "It was just a sort of waiting room. With a table and chairs, the telephone. The doctor came from next door. I didn't have a chance to see inside."

I tugged her hand gently. "How many windows in the waiting room?"

"One." She put her face against mine. "Don't go, darling. Please don't go. Somebody's bound to see you."

I wasn't too sure of it myself but I couldn't let her know it.

"It's a clinic not a bank. Let me be the expert for once. Take the car up the road as far as the clubhouse. Wait there

171

with your lights out. If I'm not back in an hour, get home as fast as you can."

She clung for one despairing second then let me go. "I'll never let you down," she said distinctly. "No matter what."

She moved the car off as I stepped into the ditch. More wire fenced the spruce plantation from the road. I went through it, brambles tearing at my trouser legs. I made no noise running over the carpet of dead bracken. It was pitch black in front of me. I had to use the flash to avoid the hazards of fallen trees. After a while I stopped to get my bearings. The cold damp air was soundless except for a trickle of water somewhere nearby. The clinic lay obliquely to my left. The quickest escape route would be from the back of the main block, where the belt of trees narrowed. A quick dash would bring me out on the road near the clubhouse. I walked on, guided by the glow through the branches ahead.

The sweep of driveway looked like the perimeter of a concentration camp, naked under the glare from the lights in the lobby. I could see the nurse sitting reading, a transistor on the desk in front of her. The windows on the left of the entrance were in darkness. I broke for the nearest one, running with my eyes on the nurse. I stood for a minute, flattened against the wall. The trees beyond the edge of the concourse drew like magnets, calling me back into shelter. The narrow window ledge was level with my chest. I put my hand on the steel frame. It didn't budge, held by a ratchet inside. The next two windows were the same. I moved along to the last one at the end of the wing. It was barely open, no more than a couple of inches. I slipped my hand through, unscrewed the catch on the ratchet and pulled the frame wide. I went

172

over the sill, closing the curtains after me. I shined the flash-light round the room. The tiny beam traveled over an oxy-gen tent, a deep sink stinking of formaldehyde, rubber gloves hanging over the dripping faucet.

A pinpoint of light glimmered through a keyhole. I grasped the handle with both hands, taking the weight of the door and opening it fractionally. A glossy white wall reflected strip lighting in the ceiling. I widened the crack. There were three rooms on each side of the corridor. The one I wanted looked a thousand miles away. At the end of the corridor was a door. A heavy metal frame held a sheet of plate glass. The nurse was sitting with her back to me. I could see the phone by her elbow.

The first cold drops trickled down my side. The nurse looked set for the night. For all I knew, she'd be there for hours. Old crafts were guiding me. Habit narrows the field of the human eye. Objects above or below the normal level of vision tend to be ignored. My move was now or never.

I buttoned my coat, dropped on my belly, and slipped out into the corridor. I wormed my way over the composi-tion flooring. I watched the woman every inch of the way. Nearer and nearer, the seconds ticking away in my stomach. I reached up and turned the handle. I rolled sideways into the room and lay perfectly still. I could hear the music from the nurse's radio. One room lay between me and the lobby. I turned the keys in both doors, walking over the carpeted floor. I opened the window, leaving the curtains drawn. The flashlight showed a cigarette gray with ash, still burning in a tray on the desk. I turned behind the beam, slowly. A wheeled filing cabinet had been pulled away from the wall.

A gap showed in the third row. I pointed the flash at the desk again. The metal rings of a folder blinked in the light. I came nearer. A typewritten label was pasted on the cover: MR. JOHN STRAIGHT.

I opened the covers, holding the flash between my teeth. The first page gave no more than his address and telephone number. The pages were shaking between my gloved fingers. I stopped turning. Two pictures were pasted into the file, a little larger than passport size and photographed with a precision lens. Under the left-hand one was written TAKEN ON RECEPTION, 17 MARCH 1967. Under the second, TAKEN ON DISCHARGE, 11 AUGUST 1967. Surgeon: *Doctor Leonard,* Anesthetist: *Doctor Crawford.*

The shape of the heads was identical. The faces could have been of different men. The later photograph was of John Straight. The other I didn't recognize. I turned the next page. The close-typed text was a case history of five months' treatment. The language was technical but four different operations were listed.

Footsteps sounded outside. I shoved the flashlight into my pocket as someone tried the handle. A man's voice called out irritably.

"Who is it keeps locking this door, nurse?"

The footsteps retreated. I heard the nurse answer and ripped the pages out of the file. I stuffed them into my coat, folded flat. Lights came on in the adjoining room. I dropped out of the window and broke for the back of the block. Elbows tight against my ribs, I took the ribbon of path, feet flying. I zigzagged behind the nurse's dormitory, into the narrow belt of spruce. Ivy whipped round my legs. The soggy bracken slowed me. The whole wood seemed to echo

174

with the racket I was making. Suddenly the road glimmered through the trees. I could see the outline of the clubhouse. Headlights flared as I neared the car. I wrenched the door open, collapsing on the seat beside Kirstie. She had the motor going. I managed one word.

"*Move!*"

The car bucketed over a pile of sand, swinging dangerously near the gate as we hit the hardtop. Kirstie put her foot down hard. I looked back through the rear window. All I could see was the glow of our taillights. She stopped at the T-junction, waiting for an oncoming car to pass. I put my hand on her knee. Her whole body was tense. My own was dead-weight. Legs gone, a dull banging where my heart was supposed to be.

"His face," I gasped. "Look at this." I had the file open at the two photographs.

She glanced down swiftly before swinging the Ford out onto the highway. The whining motor nudged the speedometer up to sixty and held there. She was sitting low in her seat, her chin just showing over the top of the steering wheel. The road unwound in the cone of light from the headlights. Her silence completely baffled me.

"Well, *say* something!" I exploded.

A truck loomed round the bend. I covered my face with my hands as she swung in to avoid it.

"For Crissakes, Kirstie," I implored.

She took her foot off the gas, dropping down to forty. I tried again, quietly and reasonably.

"Don't you understand what I'm telling you? They operated on his face. He had five months of plastic surgery."

She swallowed hard. "I saw you running. It was horrible.

You looked as that man said you would — a hunted animal."
She turned her head for a fraction of a second, long enough
for me to see the compassion in her eyes. And I knew the
truth. It was like looking at someone who fears for your
life and can do nothing more for you. It didn't matter to
her where we were going. I'd had it. And all she could do
was stay and pick up the pieces. I put the file away with the
other papers.

"You're wrong," I said doggedly. "I'll show you you're
wrong, darling. Make a right turn at the next crossroads and
follow the signs to Camberley. We're going back to Bramwell Grange."

She took a fresh grip on the wheel, her eyes welling with
tears again.

"I won't leave you," she said unsteadily. "I won't leave
you, Macbeth."

She was dangerously near hysteria. I put my hand out and
touched her. It was all I could do. The next hour was a lonely
one. We met the A3 near Ripley. Another ten minutes
brought us to the Olmer road. We turned down the lane to
the Home. The gates at the end were shut tight. I sounded
the horn and got out of the car. It was a while before the
door opened. The same woman peered out. I walked into
the glare of the headlights.

"I'm sorry to disturb you again but I've got to see Doctor
Posner."

"He's not on duty," she called back. "There's nobody
there but the night staff."

I could see the outline of the house a quarter of a mile
away. Panic made my voice shrill.

"Do you know where he is? It's urgent."

I heard her say something to someone in the lodge. A man appeared in the lighted doorway.

"Who is it? What do you want?"

I put my face close to the gates. "Is Doctor Posner there or not?"

The woman had left him to it. "He's at home. But we're not supposed to let people in, this time of night — not without notice. It's past nine o'clock."

"Phone Doctor Posner," I said. "Tell him it's about John."

"John?" he repeated doubtfully.

"That's right. He'll know. Say it's an emergency."

He went inside. He was out in a couple of minutes. He dragged the gate back, grumbling.

"First they say one thing, then another. You'll have to let yourself out and mind you put the catch up."

I climbed back beside Kirstie. "Which way do we go?"

He pointed up the drive. "Round the lake, then left. It's behind the big house. You can't miss it. You'll see the light outside."

His direction took us in a sweep through the terraced gardens to what had once been a stableyard. Loose boxes had been converted into a maisonette. A ship's storm lantern hung above the front door.

Kirstie killed the motor. She took the mirror out of her handbag and made her face presentable.

"All I want is to help," she said in a low voice.

I pulled her close to me. "It's almost over," I promised. They were the first words we'd spoken in half an hour.

We crossed the cobbled yard. I put my thumb on the doorbell. Posner looked out from behind the opening door. He was wearing a frogged velvet smoking jacket, patent leather shoes with silver buckles. His eyes settled on Kirstie curiously.

"This is a friend of mine," I said quickly. "Kirstie Kirkpatrick, Doctor Posner."

He took her by the arm. "Come in, come in."

It was a large room with chintz covers on the sofa and chairs. A log fire burned in a brick fireplace. Perched on a grand piano was the budgerigars' cage. A dated photograph beside a bowl of pot-pourri. The net round the woman's throat, her hairstyle, gave her a look of unmitigated severity. The likeness to Posner was unmistakable. He smiled, seeing my interest.

"My mother." He fluffed the cushions in the armchairs. "You here, my dear," to Kirstie. "And you here, Mr. Marlow." He piled our coats on a chair and sat down on the sofa between us. He passed the cigarette box, as elegant as an Aubrey Beardsley drawing.

"Mr. Deegan spoke of an emergency. I hope you are not bringing bad news?"

I unfastened the briefcase. "I think I'll let you decide that, Doctor. First a few questions. How much do you know about plastic surgery?"

He looked at me inquiringly. "Always the difficult questions, Mr. Marlow. I am a psychiatrist not a surgeon, remember."

Kirstie was lost in the big armchair, her face wreathed in smoke.

"You don't have to be," I answered. "I'll put it another

way. How much can plastic surgery change an individual's appearance?"

"If you mean the face," he said positively, "this can be changed completely. Many new techniques were developed during the war. Since then, many improvements. Nose, ears, chin, eyelids — even the lips — are being altered. Other characteristics can be modified. For instance the walk, by operating on the muscles of the legs or feet." Fingers strayed over his ruffled shirt.

"And how long would this take to heal?" My eyes sought Kirstie's but she was watching Posner.

His expression was puzzled. "Why are you asking me this? What connection does it have with John?"

I looked at him meaningly. "You'll know in a minute; first answer the question. How long before a patient could show himself without people knowing he's been operated on?"

He rose, shadowed against the lemon-colored wall. He bent over the cage, chirruping at the birds inside. Then he lifted his head.

"This must depend. The length of time would vary for each operation, an hour, several hours. And the healing cycles would be different. Bandages might be removed after a rhinoplasty — nose-reconstruction. It would take considerably longer for the swelling to go down. Months after a jaw operation. A complete change of facial appearance could take anything from six months to a year. Much would depend on the operations themselves, whether or not complications set in."

He stopped short as if suddenly realizing the implication of his statement.

179

"Would five months be long enough, Doctor?" I took the file out of the briefcase. "Do you recognize your patient?"

He was holding the sheet out of focus. He put his spectacles on. His expression changed to one of bewilderment.

"There must be some mistake. This is not John. It is his brother, Mark."

He was pointing at the earlier picture, the one taken in March.

Kirstie's ashtray clattered into the fireplace and broke. She made no move to retrieve the pieces. Her hand crept to her throat. Posner went down on his knees, muttering something about carelessness. He picked up the broken shards, oblivious to the bombshell impact of his announcement. My voice sounded false and theatrical.

"Would you care to swear to that?"

He climbed up, still worrying about his ashtray. Emotion thickened his accent again.

"*Swear* to it? What are you talking about!" He opened a drawer in a bureau and fished out an envelope. He spilled the contents onto the sofa and selected a snapshot. "You want to see John? Look!"

The figure was kneeling in a flowerbed, face turned toward the camera. Body and head were those of a man in his thirties. The high-speed lens had frozen the face in an expression of simple wonder — mouth open, the eyes wide and staring. The only resemblance to the other two photographs was in the shape and set of the ears. I whipped the three pictures into the briefcase and hurried to my feet. I grabbed Kirstie's coat and hustled her into it.

"Let's go," I said in her ear.

Posner stationed himself in front of the door, arms flung wide in a gesture of forbiddance.

"No!" he said excitedly. "I must not allow it. Who are you people? I must telephone the police!"

I moved him aside, waiting in the open door till Kirstie was safely in the car. Posner's arms drooped as I walked back toward him.

"Now you listen to me," I said grimly. "Call the police if you like. But it'll be the end of this institution if you do. Don't you know how detectives work on a murder investigation? They spare *nobody*, Doctor Posner. They'll interrogate your staff *and* the patients."

His face was shocked. "Murder?" he expostulated. "Who *are* you? I have the right to know."

"John Straight's dead," I said flatly. "Murdered. And you've got the same right as I have, to find the man who killed him."

His face was the color of his shirt. "Dead?" he whispered.

I made a show of authority. I didn't care what he thought as long as we got out of there.

"I'm sticking my neck out for all of you, trying to keep this place from being involved in a scandal. Don't make things any tougher for me."

He pulled himself together uncertainly, the attempt at dignity pathetic.

"I shall have to think."

"Do that," I said. "Think about your patients, Doctor. Don't do anything till you hear from the police."

I shut the door and took the wheel. We drove to the lodge without lights. I hauled the gates back, half-expecting the

181

alarm to sound in the lodge. All I heard was the noise of the television. I gunned the Ford up the road, leaving the gates wide. I put ten miles of country lanes between us and the Home and then stopped. Kirstie wrapped her arms round me, saying the same thing over and over.

"Darling, you're safe, you're safe!"

I took a deep breath and freed myself. I had a feeling that she still didn't understand the enormity of this crime.

"*They* killed him, Kirstie — Pardoe and Mark Straight. Nobody else except Redfern and the people at Bramwell had seen the poor bastard in seventeen years. Wasn't it Pardoe who identified the body as Mark's? Pardoe who set the interviews up with the bank trustees, the psychiatrists? They had everything going for them. A quarter-million pounds between them. But one killing wasn't enough for Mark. He still wanted revenge. So he killed his wife too."

"Then he *is* insane," she said in a tight voice.

I pulled the car back onto the highway. She shivered, a small shrunken figure beside me. She stared through the window at the darkness outside and spoke again, this time with decision.

"I'm coming with you."

We were on the Kingston bypass. I took the fast lane, watching the cars behind in the rear-view mirror.

"Coming *where* with me?"

"Scotland Yard."

I shook my head. "Not me. Not tonight, anyway."

She twisted in her seat, frustration and fear in her outburst. "But you've *got* to, Macbeth!" She grabbed at me. The car swerved dangerously.

I fended her off, driving with one hand. "What do you want to do, put us in the ditch? Where were the police when we needed them? I'm still on the run, Kirstie. Do you think Foster will pin a medal on me? I'll go to the Yard but not without a lawyer. And I can't do it till the morning."

"You *can*," she begged. "We can go straight to Rutley. He'll help us."

I looked at her pityingly. "Your father's solicitor? You must be out of your mind. I want someone who'll be on *my* side. Someone who knows cops don't wear haloes. First thing in the morning, Kirstie. That's a promise."

A peak of dark hair swung in front of her eyes. "Nothing I say matters, does it?" she asked brokenly. "Not even now."

Signals in front turned red. I tried to make her see reason. "You didn't believe me before, Kirstie. But believe me now. I know what I'm doing." I scribbled the Hampton Court number on a slip of paper and shoved it at her as the lights changed. "Call me at eleven tomorrow morning. The hell with the phone being tapped. I'll meet you with the lawyer and we'll go to the Yard together — if that's what you want."

She put the paper in her bag without answering. It was ten past eleven by the clock outside Chelsea Town Hall. Bitter cold had thinned the beards and bells along King's Road. A few pilgrims in Afghan goatskins clustered outside a doorway. A board there advertised readings from Ginsberg. Conventionally-clad pedestrians hurried past the psychedelic displays, heading for the steamed warmth of the clubs and the coffee bars. I turned down Dovehouse Street, found a place to park and dropped the car keys in her lap.

183

"I want you to know something. I'm still trying to be the guy you want me to be. Nothing's changed."

She blinked hard. "Why are you looking at me like that?"

"Remembering," I replied. "Just remembering."

I waited till she had locked the car and took her in my arms.

"Good night, sweetheart. I'll stay till you're safely inside. Go through the front entrance. It doesn't matter anymore. It's all over, the running and the hiding."

She lifted her face to my lips and walked off without looking back. I cut through the gate into St. Luke's churchyard, stood there till I saw the porter open the door for her. I stayed for a few more minutes, watching the street. Whoever had been tailing her, police or reporters, appeared to have called it a day. I walked north through unfrequented streets to Sloane Square.

I hadn't been bluffing. I knew exactly the man to get hold of. Phil Kaye was a junior partner in the law firm that had defended me three years previously. He was young, intelligent, and ambitious. And this time he'd have the chips to play with. I boarded a westbound train, shoving into the crush of saris and turbans. Hindustani vied with the near-Welsh babble of Jamaicans till the coach emptied at Earl's Court Station. I dropped into the nearest seat gratefully.

The bottle-nosed character sitting opposite cleared his throat. "Breed like flys, they do and don't even wash. And what about the 'ousing sitchation, what about it, eh? 'oo's bleedin' country *is* it, I'd like to know."

There were seven stops to Kingston and I didn't want to be involved. I crossed my legs and looked away. The woman sitting next to him had donned the cloak of invisibility the British assume on such occasions. He ignored her, concentrating on me.

" 'oo wants 'em here? Answer me that, will yer. It ain't you and it ain't me. It's captle . . ." The word gave him trouble. ". . . *captlests*," he finished triumphantly. " 'ere, are you listnen?"

He was forcing me to answer. "Why don't you leave me alone. I can't solve your problems," I said.

He stabbed his forefinger at me. "Course you can't and you know why? Yer a bleedin' forrner yerself!"

I moved to a seat at the end of the coach. He was still enlarging to a captive audience as I left the train. I took a bus as far as the bridge and walked up the road to the Green. The air was thick with freezing fog, the street lamps no more than fuzzed glows. I followed the curve of the wall to the gates and hurried down the driveway. A yellow pall obscured the house. I moved away from the sound of the river toward the back door. It was warm in the kitchen. I stuck the briefcase back in its hiding place under the sink. Pardoe stared up at me, blinking in the candlelight. I untied him.

"Latrine call. Don't trip on the stairs."

He limped up and down without a word. I roped him up, heated some beans, and ate them from the can. The food was a tasteless mash. I couldn't get the thought of Straight out of my mind. The quiet voice and unhurried movements, the insane confidence that drove him to achieve the unexpected. He must know by now that his file was missing from the clinic. The chances were that the staff there would put it down to a raid by an over-zealous reporter.

Straight wouldn't be likely to disillusion them. He'd certainly block any suggestion of calling in the police. His next move worried me. He was off the rails and running wild, without Pardoe's restraint or guidance.

I shut the hall door behind me and sat down at the phone. I composed Kay's number from memory. It was his wife who answered. I gave no name, just saying it was a matter of extreme urgency. I had to talk to her husband. Her voice faded, Kaye's replacing it.

"Philip Kaye speaking."

I put my mouth close to the microphone. "Have you read your newspapers — Macbeth Bain."

"I've read them," he said curtly. "Where are you speaking from?"

"I'm still in circulation. But I'm turning myself in tomorrow morning."

"So what do you want from me?" he asked cautiously.

I leaned forward, emphasizing the answer. "Help, Phil. I didn't kill this woman. I've been framed. There's all the proof you need. Make sure you get this name — John Straight — got it?"

"John Straight," he repeated. "Right. Listen, from all I hear you're in dead trouble. Do you realize that?"

"*Was*," I corrected. "Not anymore. Now you listen to *me*. The law doesn't know it but this guy is dangerous. There's a good chance he'll try to leave the country. Make sure that he doesn't. You've got contacts at the Yard."

The sound in his throat was impatient. "I can't go into a thing like this without more than you're offering, Mac. Look, I'll tell you what I'll do. Who's handling this case?"

"Somebody called Foster," I answered. "He's at the Yard, a Detective-Superintendent."

"I'll get hold of him," he said, "and arrange for your surrender. And I'll see somebody's there to protect your interests. More than that I can't do."

"I think there is, Phil," I said quietly. "Does the name Edward Pardoe suggest anything to you?"

"Pardoe?" he said quickly. "You mean the solicitor on King's Bench Walk?"

"That's who I mean." I hammered the words together. "You want more, Phil? I'm putting you on the front page of every newspaper in the country. A conspiracy to murder with a quarter-million pounds at stake. And one of the men involved, an officer of the Supreme Court."

"Where are you? Can you come here now?" he demanded.

"I couldn't cross the street," I told him. "There's thick fog where I am. Just do what you said. Arrange for me to come in tomorrow morning. I'll meet you between eleven and half past anywhere you like."

"All right," he said finally. "You remember the pub in Fleet Street? We met there the morning of your trial?"

I'd forgotten none of it. The bar crowded with solicitors. The drive with Kaye and Kirstie to surrender to my bail.

"The Four Feathers, yes."

"Then I'll pick you up there at half past eleven. And listen," he warned. "If anything happens between then and now be sure to let me know. And keep your mouth closed."

"Will do," I said. "And make sure Straight doesn't put his skates on."

The connection broke and I hung up. No one was going

to pick me up now. I was going to walk into Foster's office voluntarily. And whatever else the Fate Sisters decided, I knew this much. That I'd walk out again, this time a free man.

I crawled between cold sheets and lay there listening to Pardoe's heavy breathing.

Sunday

IT WAS STILL dark when I awoke. I looked at my watch. Twenty past seven. I went over to the window. Fingers of fog drifted between the trees. I could only just see the gate at the end of the driveway. I shaved and dressed in my own clothes. The only things in my pockets were a package of cigarettes and the money I had. I brewed some tea and went through the bathroom routine with Pardoe. This time I let him shave. He took his time, passing his fingers over his cheeks tenderly. He wiped the razor and turned round facing me. His white hair was brushed back in an imposing sweep. Except for his underwear he'd have graced any court.

"Will you allow me a cigarette?" he asked courteously.

I motioned impatiently with the gun, remembering I'd have to sink it in the river along with the keys. That much I owed Hickey.

Pardoe smiled as if he knew every secret in my mind and discounted them.

"I'm going to see you spend the rest of your life in jail, Bain. And there's nothing you can do that will stop it."

I'd promised myself I'd save it, that I'd wait till he found himself in Foster's office and watched Straight come in. But the old impulsiveness betrayed me.

189

"I could tell the police who John Straight really is," I said quietly.

I have to give him this. He still managed to hold the smile. Head and shoulders stern and resolved, eyes utterly untouchable. The bust of a Roman emperor. Something kept me smashing at the mask of pretense.

"I was in your office when you called him. Do you want me to spell it all out for you? Bramwell Grange — Hayley Memorial Clinic — George Redfern? You're through, Pardoe. Finished."

He limped past me, head erect, eyes unblinking. We were halfway down the stairs to the hall when the phone rang. I hustled him into a cupboard beneath the stairs and turned the key. I picked up the receiver. Kirstie's voice was faint.

"My God," I said. "You're only three hours early! Couldn't you sleep, darling? Never mind. It's all set. Kaye's picking me up at half past eleven. The place we met the morning of my trial — the Four Feathers on Fleet Street. Be there." A sudden thought struck me. "Is it foggy in Chelsea?"

Her whisper was almost lost. "I'm not alone, Macbeth." Suddenly Straight's voice seemed to fill the whole house. "Bain?"

I nodded as if he could see me, stunned to stupidity. "I'm here."

"Good. Then pay attention, her life is in your hands. Do you understand what I'm saying?"

The chill in his tone numbed me. "I understand," I said mechanically. Inside my brain a kaleidoscope was spinning. Kirstie walking into her flat. Straight waiting for her there.

The two of them leaving the apartment building, the porter dispatched on some errand. Mercifully, imagination stopped there.

The cupboard door was being pushed from the inside. Gently and silently.

"What do you want me to do?" I asked despairingly.

He spoke like a schoolmaster, pleased with a pupil's progress. "Much better, Bain. She's quite safe and unhurt. A little tired, perhaps and frightened but safe."

"Let me talk to her," I begged.

"If you want to see her alive," he answered significantly. "Keep away from the police. Stay where you are till I phone you again."

He couldn't know where I was. All Kirstie had was the phone number.

"How long do I have to wait?" I asked.

"I'll call you at one. And remember. She's safe only as long as I am."

He was playing for time. One short plane hop would take him to Paris or Rome. With his kind of money he could be ten thousand miles away in another forty-eight hours. The irony was that his escape routes were blocked now. And I was the one who had blocked them. Kirstie would never leave alive unless I got there first. The phone went dead.

I sat there for a moment, seeing her face, pleading and terrified. It was no good trying to have the call traced. He'd be too smart for that. The gun was still on the table. I didn't even think about it as I walked over to the cupboard. I opened the door, Pardoe came out, smoothing ruffled hair. His smile told me that he knew.

I grabbed him by the neck, sinking my thumbs into the flesh above the arteries. His mouth contorted with pain, his fingers tearing at my hands. We thrashed across the hall, banging into the furniture. I managed to pin him against the wall. A suit of armor toppled over with a crash. His face was suffused with blood, his eyes starting to roll. I let him go, heart thudding, my breathing as labored as his.

"I'll kill you, Pardoe," I promised, "if you don't tell me where she is. Where has he taken her?"

He stood there, obstinately silent, hands protecting his throat. Rage powered my arm to a knuckled swing. Each blow was for Kirstie. Blood trickled from his closed mouth. Suddenly he collapsed, to his knees first then pitched on his side. He lay in a huddle with closed eyes. I dragged him across the hall and into the cupboard. I locked the door on him again.

I sat down at the small table, staring at the phone. My whole body was shaking. I couldn't stop it. Straight wasn't bluffing. Unless I could reach her, Kirstie was as good as dead. I spun the dial. I heard the ringing tone, a click then Kaye's voice.

Each word was an effort for me. "Don't ask questions, just get here. I'm at Hampton Court, the third house on the river side of Poynders Road. It's called Heron's Lodge. And hurry."

"I'm on my way," he said quickly.

I went into the kitchen and drank a glass of water. The will to lose was dangerously strong at that moment. To give up, to accept anything they wanted to throw at me. The only thing that mattered was Kirstie's life. I cleared the remains of the breakfast and emptied the briefcase on the table. I spread the papers out, exhibits in a trial that might be too late. Time dragged on. The noise of each passing car took me to the window. If anything the fog was thicker. I had a picture of snarled traffic in shrouded streets. The whole city slowed to a walk, Kaye groping his way to a call booth. He'd phone if he couldn't get to me. That much I was sure of.

I made the beds, picked Pardoe's clothing up, went upstairs and tidied the mess I'd made in the dressing room. Anything was better than thinking. A long time seemed to go before I heard a car stop outside, the gate being dragged back. I ran down, opening the front door as Kaye's tall figure emerged from the yellow murk. He came into the hall, fashionably dressed in a gray coat with a black velvet collar. His wavy hair glistened with moisture. He looked round at the sheeted furniture then shrugged, as if nothing was left to surprise him.

"The same old Macbeth Bain. Whose house is it?"

His eyes followed mine to the cupboard beneath the stairs. His thin keen face changed expression.

"What's happened, what is it?"

"*Pardoe*," I mouthed, beckoning him into the kitchen. I closed the door. "Sit down and listen, Phil. Two people have died. The next on the list is Kirstie. Straight got hold of her last night."

He glanced through the open door at the torn sheet and cord, the one tumbled blanket I'd left on the floor.

"What do you mean, got hold of her? Where is she?"

I lifted my arms and let them fall again. "Do you think I'd be here if I knew? I watched her into her flat. He must have been there waiting. She phoned me at eight o'clock this morning. Christ knows where from but he was there with her."

He put the question sharply. "What did he say?"

I told him, the memory making my voice unsteady. "I've got to get to her, Phil. I don't care how but I've got to get to her."

"You take it easy," he warned. "Just don't panic. We've still got till one. She's going to be all right, Mac. What's this?" he added quietly. He moved the pile of papers on the table.

"The proof," I said. "The proof Foster should have found. Look for yourself."

He riffed through the documents, finishing with the three photographs. He studied them for a moment then dark eyes searched my face.

"The truth, Mac. From the beginning."

The rain-soaked library belonged to a different existence. The women in mud-spattered stockings, the old men hopelessly coughing their lungs out. I started there, making no excuse as I went through the tale of false references, burglary and abduction.

"You're a bloody fool," he said finally. "So why not come to me?"

I leaned against the dresser, looking at him. "Come to you with *what*, Phil? When I spoke to you last night, you didn't even want to act for me."

The mask slipped suddenly. The world of success forgotten. The Huntsman suits, Swedish *au-pair* girls, High Court judges bowing recognition. In one second he was a tough East End Jew ready for battle.

"OK. What about Pardoe?"

I balled my shoulders. "I don't know. He went down. I hit him hard enough. Do you want to see him?"

"The hell with him. I'll take these with me." He swept the papers back in the briefcase, leaving the gun where it was. "Get rid of this thing. The keys don't matter. There's only one thing we *can* do now — bring Foster back here. But I've got to be sure of something before I go. Will you *be* here when we get back?"

I moved away from the dresser. "Where would I go?"

He tucked the briefcase under his arm hurriedly. "Then leave things to me. Foster's expecting us at the Yard at a quarter to twelve. All he knows is what you told me last night. We need speed. It's no good using the phone. I've got to open this briefcase in front of him, light a fire under him. See you get rid of that gun while I'm gone, it never existed."

I stood at the window till the sound of his car was lost. I opened the back door. Fog billowed in the dripping trees. I went to the river's edge and slung the automatic as far as I could. It plopped into the water, somewhere out in midstream. I didn't question Kaye's instructions. He was a hard operator with a computer for a brain, a cash register for a heart. But what he promised he delivered. It was a relief to have someone else take the decisions. Back in the kitchen, I ran a bowl of water. I found a clean towel. Better to get the blood off Pardoe's face before Foster arrived, restore the image the cops liked so much. The respectable citizen who'd taken a trusting half-wit to a lonely place and used a shotgun to blow half his head off. The dignified lawyer who'd dressed the body in Mark Straight's clothing, solemnly identified it

195

and given it a suicide's burial. I had no pity for Pardoe or Straight, only fear for Kirstie.

I put the bowl of water on the floor and turned the key in the cupboard door. I must have leaned forward automatically, expecting Pardoe to be on the ground. Something swished through the air. Pain exploded at the back of my head. Then a live volcano sucked me into its crater.

The first thing I remembered was the bitterness of bile in my mouth. I pulled myself up groggily, hitting my head against the sloping ceiling. I was in the cupboard, the door locked on me. I stood back and charged it. Plaster rained down but the door still held. I braced myself stiff-armed against both walls and kicked at the lock. The door splintered away. I stumbled out into the hall. A golf club lay near the stairs where Pardoe had thrown it. A lump was growing on my neck. A couple of inches higher and my skull would have been cracked. I ran for the bedroom. Pardoe's clothes were gone. I pulled the curtain back, knowing what I'd see. The garage doors were wide.

I held my head under the faucet till the icy water numbed my temples. I dried myself and found some brandy in the dining room. I drank from the bottle and sat down, a pool of warmth invading my stomach. My head cleared slowly to un-welcome reality. I'd been there half an hour or more when the driveway filled with cars. There were three of them, police Jaguars with bloomed windows and souped-up motors.

I wrenched the front door open. Foster and Kaye jumped out of the lead car. Plainclothesmen filled the hall, trapping me in an agony of memories. The last glimpse of freedom through the window of a C.I.D. room. A cell door slamming in my face, the echo dwindling along the corridor. I walked toward Kaye's troubled face, holding my hands out.

"He jumped me — with a golf club. The car's gone."

Foster spoke quickly. "Get that number on the air. I want his flat covered and his office. And I want every call to this house monitored. Now *move!*"

One of the cops relayed the instructions to the radio operator in the lead car. Foster was wearing the same dirty mac, striped shirt, and black hat. He looked like a seedy Oriental comedian. He whistled as he saw the cupboard door. "Someone remember to notify the owner that he's had visitors," he said tersely. He put his hand on my arm, beckoning to Kaye.

He shut the kitchen door behind us. A couple of men were walking up the path toward the garage. Foster loosened his belt. He considered the state of the bedroom, his eyes inscrutable.

"Satisfied?" he said to me. "Or do you still want to go on doing my job for me?"

I went across to the sink and poured myself some more water. I drank slowly. He couldn't get off my back even now.

"I'm through," I said. "But you're going to have a whole lot to answer for if anything happens to her."

Kaye broke in quickly. "Cut it out and listen to what the Superintendent's saying."

Foster sat down. He picked the trousseau of keys up and swung them on his thumb.

"I've given Mr. Kaye my assurance, Bain. There'll be no charges against you. You're a Crown witness."

I wanted to laugh in his face. These people pulled rabbits out of their hats like conjurers. Culprit into witness — presto! Applause. I went to the heart of the matter.

197

"You've run me like a dog, Foster. Do you think I care what you do to me now? You're a cop — save her."

Foster brooded for a second. He answered as if it was important for me to believe him.

"Everything that's humanly possible is being done, Bain. With her safety in mind. But you'll have to do your share."

"*My* share!" I said incredulously. "Give me the chance — *anything!*"

Foster turned his wrist. "It's almost one o'clock. In a couple of minutes, Straight's going to phone. I want you to keep him talking. That call's got to be traced. We've gone through his flat with a fine comb. Nobody there's seen him for two days and his car's gone."

"He was there last night," I said steadily. "They called him from the clinic."

Nicotine-loaded smoke was making my head spin. I dropped the butt in the garbage pail. Someone banged on the door. Foster was up like a flash. A plainclothesman's head appeared.

"Pardoe, sir. They just missed him at his office. He'd only been gone minutes. He's still using his car. Control's waiting for news of it."

"*Waiting?*" Foster hammered him with the words. "What do they think this is, a Band of Hope meeting? I want that car traced. And tell them to keep well away from it. He's not to know he's being followed. Leap-frog him!"

I'd seen the technique in action. A relay of police vehicles would be strung out ahead of a suspect. Cars, trucks, delivery wagons, motorcycles. One after another would take up the chase. The phone rang and Foster shoved me into the hall.

198

I picked up the receiver. It was Straight, his voice remarkably clear.

"Bain? Listen to me carefully. Stay where you are. I'll phone you again at six. You'll be told where to come."

Foster was leaning over my shoulder, mouthing the words at me. *Keep him talking!*

"Am I going to need transport?" I asked. "There's thick fog here."

Nobody answered. The connection was already broken. Foster ran to the open door. The choking yellow murk was drifting into the hall. The radio operator in the lead car stuck his head out of the window.

"They've traced the call, sir. An A.A. box near the junction of the A24 and the A283. It's near a place called Aldbourne."

"That's *it!*" The table went as I came to my feet. "The house they took for the nurse!"

I ran for the door. Foster trapped me halfway in an arm lock. "The name of the house!"

I wrenched myself free. "I don't know. A vicarage, I think. But Aldbourne I'm sure about."

He swung round, barking instructions at the men at the foot of the stairs.

"You two stay here. If anyone puts a nose past that gate, hang on to them. I don't care who it is, nail 'em."

His hand was in the small of my back, urging me into the first car. We piled into the rear, three of us. Foster was in the middle. The man sitting on the other side of him was stolid-faced and had a heavy cold. The rest of the cops crowded into the other two cars, Kaye somewhere among them. Foster leaned forward, flicking his fingers for the microphone.

"Charley-six to Control, over."

The speaker crackled on the dashboard. "Control to Charley-six, over."

Foster lurched as the car hit the rise. "Notify all units concerned. Quarry believed to be heading for Aldbourne. That's a couple of miles west of Ashington on the A24. Do not intercept. I repeat. Do *not* intercept."

He slumped back with his chin on his chest. The cortège of cars shot the bridge and took a south-easterly line. The driver touched a switch. The oscillating wail of the siren sent the traffic scurrying for the curb. Visibility was no more than thirty yards but the three cars maintained their steady speed. We burned one set of signals after another, sirens wailing. Trucks loomed from the gloom, blurred headlights appearing with sickening suddenness. I shut my eyes a dozen times, a crash seeming inevitable. We drifted out of danger at the last split second. The driver's jaws worked methodically. The smell of his gum permeated the car. Radio reports were coming in regularly, plotting Pardoe's course with relentless persstence. Fog warnings. An account of a multiple crash blocking the highway outside Redhill.

Foster took the mike again, spitting the words. "You can cut out the light information. Where's EP 100?"

A voice droned an answer. "EP 100 approaching Reigate traveling at thirty-five miles an hour. No sign of alarm. Over and out."

An ordnance map was spread across Foster's lap. He traced our line with a nicotine-stained finger. We were gaining ground on Pardoe, five miles north of him on a parallel highway. Foster ringed a spot on the map, lifting his head up.

200

"What about the local force?"

The radio operator twisted in his seat. "Surrey's given us clearance. West Sussex is standing by for your instructions."

Foster grunted and undid his mac. The map slipped to the floor. A Webley forty-five sagged from a holster round his middle. He pulled it out, feeling the weight in his hand.

"How long since you fired one of these things, Harry?"

The man with the cold sniffed heavily. I saw the outline of his own gun, a bulge in his pocket.

"I dunno. About six months, isn't it? You were on the same course with me. Marksmanship, remember?"

Foster slid the weapon back in its holster. "That's right, Marksmanship. I got four out of five at twenty yards. Misses."

He picked the map up again, his eyes hidden in their puffed folds. The inscrutable East. It was a tight fit on the back seat. I wriggled an arm free to give myself a light. I'd left without an overcoat. Jacket and trousers was all I was wearing. The fog was denser here but the driver showed no sign of having noticed it. The speedometer needle was glued to the fifty mark. He'd turned off the siren. No one in the car spoke. The only sound other than the motor was the whine of the tires on the wet road.

For the first time I started thinking beyond the hazards of crashes and skids. The glimpse of the guns was a reminder of how seriously Foster rated the expedition. Weapons were only issued in an emergency. I wasn't even sure what I was doing in the car. Foster hadn't spoken to me since we'd left the house. In fact, no one had spoken to me.

A new voice echoed in the speaker. "Panda one-zero calling Charley-six, over."

The operator passed the mike back over his shoulder. Foster spoke curtly.

"State your position and go ahead, Panda one-zero."

"We're in Aldbourne, sir. In the car park, outside the Rising Sun. EP 100 has just gone into a house a hundred yards away. Just the driver in the car. We've had someone down there. You can't get near to the house without being seen — not even with the fog. Instructions, please. Over."

A vein was working near Foster's temple. "Keep away from the bloody house! Do you hear that, keep away! I've got your position. The road's marked as a dead end. Correct?"

"Right, sir. Panda-eleven's covering it from the other end."

Foster steadied himself. We were swinging left past scattered farm buildings.

"Charley-six to all units. I am approaching Aldbourne from the A23. Maintain your stations and do not approach the house. I'll be there in a few minutes. Out." He touched the driver's shoulder. "Pull up here." Brakes squealed behind us. Foster climbed out over my legs and walked back to the other cars. They flashed by, one after another. I had a brief glimpse of Kaye sitting in the back of the first.

Foster took his seat again. He folded the map into a small square. Aldbourne was plumb in the center. The road forked, left to Ashington, right, the dead end through the tiny village. The only building marked on the map was a church. We rolled off onto a parking lot. The sign on the end of the whitewashed wall was just discernible: THE RISING SUN BRICKWOOD'S ALES. The windows of the inn were lit but

202

there was no sign of life. Cattle lowed in the field behind us, a desolate sound muffled by the yellow-gray pall that hung over us. Foster leaned over and wound down my window. He called across to the police car parked close to the wall.

"Which side's the house, left or right?"

The cop at the wheel stuck his arm out. "About a hundred yards down on the left, sir. Beyond the church. You can't see it from here. It lies well back from the road. There's a lane between it and the churchyard."

Foster stared into the gloom. "No trees, no cover?"

The cop was speaking to someone behind him. He answered hesitantly.

"I've got the local constable here, sir. If you want to talk to him."

Foster's shoulders blocked the window. "Well what are you waiting for, an introduction?"

A thick-set man lumbered over, touching the peak of his uniform cap.

"Police-Constable Skinner, sir."

"What's the layout of this place?" demanded Foster. "How far is it from the church? Is there a back way in?"

I could smell the lozenges on the man's breath. He answered with a countryman's ponderousness.

"There *isn't* but one way in, sir. Round the front. It's the old vicarage, you see. The road drops sharpish by the church and there's a twenty-foot bank round the house with barbed wire on top. They used to breed terriers — least, Mrs. Ellis did."

"All right, all right." Foster broke in impatiently. "Better take a look, Harry. See if there's a chance of getting people

203

into that churchyard. I'll stay, in case there's a call. There's got to be a gate or something. I'll bring that other car up nearer. We may have to rush them."

I grabbed at his sleeve. "Are you out of your mind — Kirstie's in there!"

He sat very still, looking at me. "Will you take your hands off me, please?" The two men in front turned, ready for action. I took my hand away, pleading.

"Don't I have the right to make a suggestion?"

His jaw muscles relaxed. "That you do."

I took the rubber-molded flashlight from the shelf behind us. I pulled the doorhandle open, one foot already outside. I could hear the hidden cattle lowing nearby. Twenty yards and I'd be lost.

"I can make that house without being seen. Send one man with me. You can roll down the hill with the motor switched off. Stop by the churchyard. They won't be able to see you from the house. I'll signal whoever comes with me as soon as I'm sure Kirstie's safe. Do what you like then."

He looked at me searchingly and then shrugged. "It might work. You go with him, Harry. Do what he says. And watch yourselves," he added tersely.

We started down the road, guided by a low wall in front of cottages. A dog barked as we passed. I heard it race across the garden and thud against the fence, whining and snuffling. My partner was walking as if his shoes were spring-loaded. From time to time he wiped his running red nose on the sleeve of his gun hand. The road descended steeply, the bank already higher than our heads. We climbed steps cut into the side. A gate green with mold creaked open. Tombstones dripping with moisture sagged in the untended grass. A notice over a padlocked alms box in the porch read ALDBOURNE PARISH CHURCH, *Evensong on 2nd and 4th Sundays at 6:30 p.m. from May to October.* .

The church door was open. The nave ran parallel with the road, the altar facing east, on our right. A brass cross glimmered in front of the stained glass windows. Hassocks and hymnals were piled on the pews. It was bitterly cold. The vestry room was empty and smelled of mildew. An outside door opened onto the northern half of the churchyard. I looked out through the dirty window. There was a small gate in the wall twenty yards away. Beyond the intervening lane, the vicarage garden sloped down to the tangle of mesh and barbed wire. The house showed hazily. One yellow patch of light shone in an upstairs window. The cop grunted behind me.

"You won't have a chance, mate. If you can see them, they can see you."

I pushed past him and unbolted the door. "*Nobody's* going to see me. Keep your eyes on the back door."

I slipped out, ducking low between the tombstones. I crouched in the shelter of the wall and looked back. I could just see the cop's face behind the window. Fog billowed in the lane, trapped between the steep banks. By now Foster should be at the junction. The relayed signal would reach him in seconds. I trotted up the lane. There *was* only one place to gain the garden — the open gate on my right. A strip of hardtop snaked round to the other side of the house.

Ivy covered the walls to the guttering. The ground-floor windows facing me were protected by iron bars. The lighted window was curtained but I went through the gate with a feeling of being watched. A crow croaked somewhere off on the left, a rasping noise like a saw going through hardwood. I followed the sound through clumps of dead chrysanthemums. A couple of elms loomed in the fog. A limp towel hung on the line stretched between them. Two cars were parked in front of the house. The Bentley and Straight's Mercedes.

I dashed the twenty yards, flattening myself against the dripping ivy. It was quiet. Almost too quiet. I inched along to the front door. Unlocked. I edged in cautiously. The hall floor was carpetless, the wainscoting scarred by clawmarks. There was an ancient smell of dogs and a shotgun case on the table. It was empty.

I knew now why Pardoe had gone to his office. He'd known all along where to find Straight, and gambled that my fear for Kirstie would keep me away from the police. Straight would never leave this house alive. A body would be found fifty miles away in a field somewhere, the shotgun beside it. A short-range blast would have multilated the head beyond recognition. John Straight — Mark Straight. It wouldn't matter anymore. There'd be nothing left but conjecture. Pardoe would make sure that someone in his office remembered Straight collecting the shotgun. He'd have the weight of wealth going for him and a lifetime's knowledge of criminal law. Only one person could testify that he'd been here with Straight. And she wasn't meant to leave the house alive either.

I could hear Pardoe's voice directly overhead. The words were unrecognizable but the tone was bitter with denuncia-

206

tion. My feet made no sound crossing the hall to a dim white-washed passage leading to the back door. I drew the bolts carefully, dragging the door back. A pad of wet leaves came with it. Beyond the snarled wire at the bottom of the garden was the vague shape of the wall and the church.

Every step I took carried Kirstie's life with it. Surprise was my only hope. I groped my way into the kitchen. Enough light filtered through the windows for me to make out the old-fashioned dresser and stove. A metal wrench hung on a rail. I slipped it into my pocket, looking for the fuse box. I found it with the main switch in a cobwebbed closet full of broomsticks.

I went up the stairs to the dim landing, close to the wall, the wrench in my hand. A strip of light showed at the bottom of a door along the passage. It was Straight's voice now, urgent with argument. I backed off, trying the doorhandles behind me as I went. The second was locked. I turned the key, going in quickly behind the opening door. A figure moved in the darkness. I had my hand over Kirstie's mouth before she could make a sound. She was naked except for bra, stockings and pants. Streaked mascara mapped her cheeks. I held her shaking body fiercely.

"*Clothes,*" I whispered.

She shook her head. I ripped a blanket from the bed and covered her with it. My mouth was still close to her ear.

"I'm going to cut the light. As soon as I do, start running. The police are outside. OK?"

She made a token gesture of obedience. I catfooted back down to the kitchen. The power switch went down. A shot rang out upstairs. Then I heard Kirstie stumbling down. I

207

ran for the darkened hall, dragged her along the corridor and pushed her through the door. I started signaling frantically with the flashlight. She was running painfully, grit grinding into her stockinged feet, the blanket flapping. Suddenly she was out of sight, hidden by the slope of the bank.

The cold rage in my mind had nothing to do with heroics. All I wanted was to punish and destroy. I edged back along the passage, still gripping the wrench. Pardoe was waiting for me at the foot of the stairs. The shotgun barrels lifted slowly, till they were level with my chest. Time seemed to freeze us in a prelude of violence. His eyes were merciless. I was afraid but hatred was stronger than fear. I dropped the wrench and started toward him. He backed away till the wall brought him up short. The gun jerked and I hurled myself sideways. The edge of the blast took me high in the right shoulder, spinning me toward the stairs. My ears were deafened by the explosion, my nose filled with the stink of cordite.

The front door burst open. More cops flooded in from the kitchen passage, Foster at their head. Pardoe vanished in a mêlée of flying arms and legs. I grabbed at the banister rail. Blood was running down my sleeve, seeping through my clenched fingers. Kirstie's face came out of the haze. I took one step towards her. She caught me as I fell.

When next I opened my eyes, I was lying on a couch under a bright light, naked to the waist. My right arm was strapped to my chest. It was without feeling. The smells and sounds of a hospital surrounded me. A Hindu in a surgical smock helped me up to a sitting position and held a glass to my lips.

I gagged on the bitter liquid and pushed it away. I put my feet to the ground, groggily.

He was a short man, heavily pockmarked. "All these pellets, man, I've taken out of your body and you don't say thank you?"

The smell of the place was making me want to retch. And suddenly I saw her, miraculously there against the glossy white wall, her clothes retrieved, her eyes tender. She came toward me, holding my bloodstained jacket.

"Straight?" I said unsteadily.

She shook her head. "He's still in the operating room. They say he won't live."

The Hindu was at the sink, washing his hands. She spoke to his reflection.

"Can he go now, Doctor?"

He turned round, nodding. "But I have to know where you're taking him, that arm will need watching."

Challenge flared in her face. She wrapped the jacket round my shoulders, holding on to an empty sleeve.

"I'm taking him home," she said distinctly.

He was still muttering in Hindustani as we walked out to the waiting police car.

>>> If you've enjoyed this book and would like to discover more great vintage crime and thriller titles, as well as the most exciting crime and thriller authors writing today, visit: >>>

The Murder Room
Where Criminal Minds Meet

themurderroom.com